Johnny and the Mystery of the Rusty Musket

By Dr. Patrick Johnston

Illustrated by Nicole Zubro

PRESS

Copyright © 2012 by Dr. Patrick Johnston

Johnny and the Mystery of the Rusty Musket
By Dr. Patrick Johnston
Illustrated by Nicole Zubro

Printed in the United States of America

ISBN 9781619964549

www.xulonpress.com

Dedication

As a father of eight homeschooled children, I'm always looking for ways to entertain my children while strengthening their faith and imparting a vision for greatness. I want to place the heroes of history before them and prod them past the mountains those pioneers trail-blazed to even greater exploits.

My four oldest children – Charity, Anna, James, and Daniel – are the heroes and heroines of this novel. Their feats transcend reality in fantastic ways, but their courageous exploits are not out of reach, even for children. God's eyes always roam to and fro, looking to show Himself strong on behalf of those whose hearts are perfect toward Him. He is able to "do exceedingly abundantly above all that we can ask or think, according to the power that worketh in us" (Eph. 3:20).

My children, this novel is dedicated to you. Know the Lord. Pray without ceasing. Praise Him at all times. Fear no one but God. Defend the poor and helpless. Preach boldly. Expand the kingdom everywhere. Charge the gates of hell. Conquer in Jesus' name. Your faith is the victory that overcomes the world.

Chapter 1

"**G**et up, slave! The time for your execution draws near." When Princess Anna was slow to jump up at the slave master's word, the cruel tyrant waved her stick overhead and threatened to bring it down upon the scalp of the captured princess. "Now!"

The slave master thought she heard the erratic cracking of branches through the dense forest up the hill. She turned to study the shadows for any sign of the most feared warrior in the entire kingdom. "Please, no." She gasped. "The Vigilante must have caught our scent."

Princess Anna's eyes lit up and a hopeful smile crept upon her fear-struck countenance. "The Vigilante?"

They suddenly heard the harsh sound of the whacking of wood against wood in the distance, obnoxious, fearless, and dangerously close. Their eyes darted toward the racket.

"The Vigilante!" the princess squealed.

The slave master commanded in a gravelly voice, "Quiet!" She grabbed the princess by the scruff of her frilly white dress and pulled her under some overhanging brush down a deer trail.

"No!" screamed Anna.

In the shadows, James "the Vigilante" gripped the stick as though it were a real sword and not simply an imaginary prop in one of the Johnston children's favorite games, "Slave."

Seven-year-old Daniel's keen eyes scoured the trees for the source of the screaming. His big brother James swung his thick stick against the ground and against fallen branches for the pure joy of it, making too much noise to hear anything except the whistling and growling of his sword-fighting sound effects. James' mind had wandered from rescuing Princess Anna to his own imaginary battle. The bark and mulch that scattered through the air with each swing of his thick stick was blood and shrapnel from his little personal Armageddon. His head full of orange-red hair fit his aggression like a hand would fit a custom glove.

James paused to glance at Daniel, preparing to command him into his imaginary fray. When he saw Daniel's ear tilted toward the wind, he remembered the missing Princess. James knew that his little brother was either too entertained or too intimidated at the sight of his fierceness to urge him to be quiet so he could locate the kidnapped daughter of the African King.

James pointed at his little brother with his razor-sharp Samurai sword, and spoke in a bellowing voice, "What do your elf-ears hear, Captain Daniel?"

"I think I heard them over there." Daniel pointed across a small wooded valley.

"We must rescue the princess!" A few great leaps down the trail and James disappeared through the trees, leaving Daniel struggling to keep up. At the bottom of the hill, they saw Charity "the slave master" tying Princess Anna to the Big Oak, where executions were performed. James quietly darted from tree to tree as he snuck up on them.

Charity, the eldest Johnston child, held her imaginary torch high. "Prepare to die!" She lowered the torch to light the wood under the condemned slave when James burst through the bushes and landed on his feet right in front of her.

"Attack!" James lunged at her with a skillful swing of his sword, which Charity ducked.

"It's the Vigilante!" nine-year-old Anna's gleeful squeal echoed through the trees.

A vicious sword fight commenced, complete with blood-curdling exclamations and witty one-liners as the Vigilante repelled the slave master with some quick-footed vigor and too-close-for-comfort sword swings. Charity retreated into the shelter of the trees, out of the reach of the master swordsman.

Charity threw a warning over her shoulder as she hopped down the hill, her long, red hair bouncing in her wake, "I shall return for my rightful property!"

Further down the slope, she ducked behind a tree. She saw James bend to untie the princess. Captain Daniel, prodded on by the merciless ambition of the Vigilante, bounded down the hill as fast as his asthma would allow him.

James placed his hands on the sides of his mouth to amplify his voice. He shouted encouragement to his little brother. "Get the slave master, Captain Daniel!"

Charity leaped back into the open and headed down toward the creek, graciously slowing her pace to give Daniel a fighting chance.

"I can't." Daniel took a deep breath between asthmatic coughs. The fallen leaves of Ohio's breezy November brought out the worst in Daniel's allergies. "I can't..."

James and Anna were right behind Daniel, hoping to get a glimpse of the bitter end of the American slave trade.

Charity ducked behind a tree, and Daniel ran past her. When James and Anna neared, Charity's insides bubbled with adrenaline. She jumped out into the trail and startled her siblings with a boisterous exclamation, "The South has risen again!" Charity grabbed Anna by the hand and began to run down a steep deer trail toward the creek, dragging her giggling sister behind her. Charity didn't have James' leathery aggression, but she could definitely outwit him and outrun him.

James let out a violent growl and hopped down the steep trail in the slave master's wake. Charity's long legs cleared a narrow area of the creek, but Anna tripped and fell into the four-inch deep water, landing on her shoulder.

"Ow!" Anna grabbed her shoulder in pain.

Charity hardly had time to check on Anna's injuries when James jumped a blackberry bush and landed right into the center of the shallow creek, splashing everybody with the chilly spray. "Prepare to meet your Maker!" He held his sword at the ready against Charity's. Charity did not retreat as usual, but gave a quick thrust of her stick and struck James right in the stomach.

"Gotcha!" Charity stepped back, her face beaming in the glory of a rare victory against the Vigilante.

Charity saw James' face emanate fury. She knew that it was hard for James to take defeat graciously. "No," James protested as he shook his head, "I got you first!"

Charity and Anna simultaneously reproved their brother, "That's a lie!"

James' face grew hot and Charity pitied him, knowing that his conscience must be flogging him with guilt. "James!" Charity aimed an index finger at him. "You've gotten in trouble more for lying than anything! When are you gonna learn?"

"You're right," he confessed as he humbly bowed his head with shame. "You got me first."

Daniel moseyed up to the creek bank, coughing and wheezing. Anna, the most tenderhearted of the four, pitied him. "Are you okay, Daniel? Need a breathing treatment? You can ride on my back to the house."

Charity's eyes rolled to the treetops and she shook her head condescendingly. "Daniel can't ride on your back to the house, silly."

"Yeah, I'd squish you like a worm." Daniel glanced at the dark clouds overhead. "It looks like it's gonna rain. We should head back."

Something in the creek bed caught Charity's eye, and she bent down to investigate. "Check it out. This is what you tripped on, Anna." Charity wrapped her hands around a rusty pole that protruded from the ground at an angle. "Hey guys, help me pull this thing up! Maybe it's a lever that opens a secret underground bunker that holds the Ark of the Covenant." She unleashed a contagious grin that invited her siblings into her fantasy.

"Yeah." Daniel bent down to help his sister pull on the rusty metal pole.

James put his hands on his hips. "Charity, we ain't gonna find—"

"Aren't." Anna corrected her little brother as she sat up on the side of the bank, her right hand cupping her painful left shoulder.

James bit his lip to keep from snapping back at his big sister. He wearied of being corrected. "We *aren't* going to find the ark in our woods."

"It's wiggling a little bit." Charity grunted as she pulled on it. "Come on guys. Help us pull this magic lever up."

James glared disapprovingly at his big sister. "Magic's of the devil, Charity."

"That's right," Daniel said. He was always in James' "Amen

corner" when James got to preaching about something.

Charity rebutted. "But you always pretend about killing people with your fake swords and fake guns."

James' face reddened. "Only bad guys like murderers and Goliaths and Muslim terrorists. If good people are doin' it in the Bible, it ain't sin."

"Isn't," Anna corrected him again.

"So there, you agree with me," James teased, with mischief in his bright blue eyes.

"Anna!" Charity ignored her brother's rebuttals and addressed her sister sternly. "Stop trying to be the 'Home-schooled Grammar Student of the Year' and help us with this pole."

"It's moving!" Ecstatic, Daniel shouted loud enough for every rodent within a half a mile to wet itself out of fear. That boy had one volume, and if wasn't worth screaming at the top of his lungs, it wasn't worth saying. "The pole's moving!"

"I'm cold." Anna wrapped her arms around her chest and shivered. Her shirt, wet from her fall into the creek, clung stubbornly to her skin. "Y'all are irritatin' me. I'm heading back to the house." Her face transformed into a gloomy smirk as she started up the trail that led to their home.

The soil around the rusty pole finally gave way and they lifted it out of the thick black mud.

"Whoa!"

"Check it out!"

"Cool!"

"What?" Anna turned around to see what had so excited her siblings.

"It's an old gun!" James bent close to examine the long rifle. He scratched the mud off the stock with his fingers, and then pulled his sister's fingers away from the trigger. "Dad said to never touch the trigger unless you're ready to shoot whatever it is the gun's pointin' at."

"It's all rusted, James," Charity responded. "Even if it does have a bullet in it, the gunpowder's surely decomposed in all this damp dirt. It's a flintlock rifle, the kind they used in the Civil War."

"Look." Daniel pointed at the butt of the stock. "It's got a name on it. J-O-H...."

Charity scraped the mud off the bottom of the stock with greater care, and read the engraving out loud. "Johnny. This gun belonged to someone named Johnny."

Anna returned to inspect the finding. She bent down to look closely at the stock. "Yep. 'Johnny'."

"I read it first," Daniel reminded them with a cheesy smile.

Anna reached for the ancient weapon, and the moment they all placed their hands on the gun at the same time, the sky went black as night. The breath was snatched out of their lungs as if by a vacuum. In the next instant, the night turned as bright as the sun. The blinding light hurt their eyes and made them shrink back from the sky in fear.

The yellow, red, and brown leaves on the ground around them were sucked up into the air and began to swirl around them. The four children huddled together, gasping in horror. The wind threw the girls' hair in every direction. They could hardly open their eyes for the swarm of wind and leaves that sprinted around them as fast and strong as a herd of wild stallions frightened by an angry rattler. A bright cherry smell stung their noses, like a warm Christmas-scented candle. It was a smell that strangely warmed them in the midst of the chaos all around. Hot, humid air slapped at their faces, like the gust from the oven when Mom's cookies finished baking. Soon, the wind and leaves became a yellow haze, an impenetrable wall of unnatural fury.

James and Daniel cried out fearfully with the roar of the elements. Charity and Anna looped their arms over their brothers' shoulders and hugged them close.

"We're in a tornado!" Charity pulled her siblings toward the ground. "Duck down! Quick!" The three oldest shrunk down to the bank of the creek, their hands and knees sinking into the soft, wet soil. Daniel, however, spurned his sister's wisdom and stood up to try to escape the raging roar of the whirlwind and the swirling leaves.

"Daniel!" Anna cried out to him. "Get down!"

Daniel first reached for the wall of wind, leaves, and chaotic motion, and then stepped closer to it.

"No!" James cried out and reached for Daniel as Daniel bravely thrust his right arm through the wall of wind and leaves. Immediately, the sound decreased and the colorful blur gradually slowed. The leaves began to fall erratically to the ground. They looked up and saw the sky above them; it was baby blue, not the dreary gray of the damp Ohio fall. As the leaves floated to the ground around them, they saw that they were not in the woods anymore. This was the high point of a field that stretched for hundreds of yards in every direction. The grass beneath their feet was thick and green, and a ring of brown, yellow, and red leaves encircled them on the ground – the only leaves in the vast field. The sun was rising fast and the misty air was thick with humidity.

"What in the world?!" Charity's voice was high-pitched, teeming with anxiety. "What happened?"

"The rusty gun!" James pointed at Charity's right hand. "It's a slingshot now."

Charity hoisted the leather straps into the air and studied it. "How'd that happen?"

"That's one of them old-timey slingshots." Daniel moved closer to look at it.

"Yeah, that no one can shoot worth a flip." Charity threw it on the ground in frustration. "None of us could hit the broadside of a dinosaur with that worthless contraption."

"Hold on, Charity." James twitched his nose nervously as he studied the twisted straps of leather on the ground. He reached down to pick up the leather sling. "We don't know where we are or what's going on, but freakin' out isn't gonna make anything better." He folded the slingshot and stuffed it in his front pocket.

Daniel squinted toward the horizon. Charity saw the concerned look on his face. "What is it Daniel?"

"Somebody's comin'."

Four huge soldiers, carrying spears and shields, wearing head and chest armor, pierced a layer of fog that clung stubbornly to the ground, heading right toward them.

Charity's eyes widened as they approached. "Run!" She pointed at a tree line she could barely discern through the mist a hundred yards away.

"They may be friendly, wait." Overly curious in the face of the unknown, James shielded his eyes with his hands from the brightness of the rising sun to get a better view of the approaching soldiers. "Maybe they can tell us where we are."

"No thank you." Charity put her hands on her hips and wagged her head critically. "That's your 'pick-up-the-snake-to-see-if-it's-poisonous' strategy, and it's a recipe for disaster. Let's run!"

"No, wait," said James.

Daniel saw that there weren't four soldiers, but hundreds of soldiers marching in four lines. "There's a whole bunch of them."

"Hey!" James waved his hands to get their attention. "Hey there!"

"James, you need to listen to Charity." Anna had an anxious tremor in her voice that began to worry the emotionally malleable Daniel.

"Ah, it's all right." James continued to wave his arms over his head. "Hey, over here!"

* * * * *

The famed general was not in a good mood. This conflict was taking much longer than anticipated to win. His superiors were getting impatient. They wanted a striking victory and they wanted it today.

The general caught sight of four people of short stature at the top of the hill. By the bright color of their hair, they certainly were not Philistines.

"Halt!" The general waved his hand authoritatively and the soldiers immediately complied and stood at attention. He was two feet taller and a hundred pounds heavier than the largest soldier in his company.

"Scope." He stretched his hand toward a subordinate and the bearded Philistine warrior dropped an expanding brass scope into the general's palm. The general expanded the scope and spied the four suspicious characters at the top of the hill. They dressed rather irregular and appeared young. Two taller females and two shorter males. Two redheads and two blondes. His suspicion aroused. He sensed a trap. In times of warfare, it is safer to kill than to let a lingering doubt cloud your confidence. He collapsed the scope and handed it back to the subordinate.

"Who are they, General?"

"Appetizers for Dagon's feast on the morrow. Apprehend and interrogate them."

"Yes General."

* * * * *

"I don't think they're friendly." Charity grasped to Daniel's hand. "Let's head for the woods."

"Since when do soldiers attack little kids in Ohio?" James tried to calm down his fearful siblings.

"Yeah." Daniel nodded, encouraged by James' fearlessness. "We'll whessle 'em and beat 'em up." Daniel brought a right uppercut into an imaginary chin of an imaginary enemy. "We'll whoop 'em like Bob."

Frustration made Charity's voice sharp and her brow furrowed. "Bob is a rubber punching bag in our basement who doesn't fight back, Daniel. I don't think those guys will stand still and let us practice karate kicks on them."

James spurned Charity's tendency to fear and he looked at Daniel and grinned ear to ear. "Everything's fine. We just need to find out where we—"

Before James could finish his sentence, a spear suddenly struck the ground right between his feet.

"What!" James gasped as the significance of that ten-foot-long, ankle-thick spear began to sink in.

"Run!" Charity shouted, turning and sprinting for the tree line.

The three younger Johnston kids were right on her heels.

"We can't outrun—" A cough cut short Daniel's shout. The words on his shirt – "Jesus saves" – expanded and contracted with each deep wheezy breath.

James' confidence had been replaced with fresh fear: "We've got to try."

* * * * *

"They're fleeing into Israelite territory, General." The soldiers slowed as the hill grew steep before its crest. Their chests heaved with exertion and their muscular bodies glistened with sweat.

"Capture them! Or I'll eat your hearts with garlic and cloves for dinner!" The ruthless general raised his voice to be heard over the clanging of his troops' heavy armor.

"Yes, General Goliath." The captain called out his three fastest runners, "Grissel, Knotten, and Leffander." The warriors immediately broke out of line and ran up beside him and their famed general. "Run ahead and capture those Jewish weasels."

Chapter 2

Halfway to the tree line, Charity looked over her shoulder and calculated that the soldiers would intercept them before they could disappear into the cover of the trees. The huge warriors continued to gain on them.

"Come on, Daniel!" Anna slowed to accommodate his asthma and hold his hand.

James made it to the cover of the woods first, leaping over a fallen tree. Charity was right behind him.

"Hurry, Daniel!" Anna hoisted him over the fallen tree. Daniel leapt over its branches into the arms of Charity and James.

"Anna!" Charity's shrill scream chilled them all to the bone. "Duck!"

Anna turned and saw a ten-foot long sharp spear coming right at her head. She ducked in the nick of time and the spear stuck in the two-foot thick limb of a fallen tree. A second spear pierced her blue jean skirt and fastened the fabric to the ground. It only nicked her thigh, but she found herself unable to move. Anna removed her pocketknife to cut her skirt so that she could free herself, but three of the soldiers quickly descended upon her, their spears cocked as they prepared to impale her.

"Don't move!" one of them shouted at her in a strange accent.

Charity's heart sunk into her stomach when she realized that her sister's life was in danger. "Anna!"

Anna turned her gaze to where her brothers and sisters hid behind the dry gray branches of a low hanging olive tree. Her eyes met Charity's. "Run Charity! I'm not going to make it."

"No!" Charity stood to protest, and then ducked to dodge a spear that was headed right for her chest. The spear struck the tree behind her, the long sharp blade completely disappearing into the trunk from the force of the throw.

"Come on! They're gonna kill us!" James grabbed Daniel's hand and zigzagged away from the shower of spears that rained down upon them. "Charity!" he screamed between hurried breaths. "Run! Or we're gonna get run through like shish-ka-bobs!"

Anna screamed as the soldiers threw several more spears in the direction of the fleeing children. "No! Leave them alone!" Her breathing rate quickened as fear caused her head to swoon and her hands to tingle. The soldiers stopped and stared in wonder at the blonde-headed girl who pointed a small pocketknife at them, gritting her teeth angrily.

"Check out this little pest." The nearest Philistine plucked the spear out of the ground, freeing Anna. "I'll take that little bark-scraper of yours." He reached for the fragile girl's knife.

Anna stepped quickly inside his reach and aimed a kick at his groin. The man did not suspect such quick aggression, and he fell to both knees in pain. Anna swung her little knife at the soldier's face and another soldier caught her wrist just in time, her knife having made only a small nick in the injured soldier's cheek. With the soldier's thick hand rightly wrapped around her fragile right wrist, Anna's impromptu escape plan faded away like a snowflake in the Sahara.

"Feisty!" The soldier wrapped his hairy, muscular arms around her neck. "Oooh, I'd love to snap this little lamb's head off her shoulders like a cork off a bottle of brew." The other soldiers laughed as Anna's eyes began to dim and she came to the brink of unconsciousness.

"The general said he wants at least one of them alive." The captain came upon the scene and the soldier who was choking Anna grunted and let her go. She fell to her hands and knees, gasping for air.

Anna climbed to her feet and tearfully belted, "Leave me alone!" The soldiers were amazed at the child's audacious disrespect for her conquerors. The soldier who had choked her tried to grab her wrist and twist it behind her back when she stomped hard on the man's sandal-clad foot. He loosed his grasp and she thrust her head forward and then backward, smashing the soldier's nose with the back of her head.

"Ow!" he groaned as the blood began to trickle down his face.

Anna turned to make a break for the woods when she felt a tremendous force against the side of her face.

Smack!

She sat up, dizzy, and saw a huge, nine-foot-tall warrior standing over her. With the sun behind him shining into her eyes, she felt like an ant about to be baked by a cruel bully with a magnifying glass. The man's arms were as thick as an elephant's leg, and his skin was as hairy as a horse. A disgusting blast of his skunk-breath almost made Anna gag, but she didn't dare react when she saw the viper-like glare in his beady black eyes.

The general mocked his men. "What kind of pathetic warriors are you?!" Spit flew from the corner of his mouth and settled on his wide, black beard as he screamed. His right hand rested on the sheath of a three-foot long dagger at his belt, and his other hand gripped a wide, gleaming sword that was as long as Anna was tall. She thought her eyes were playing tricks on her when she saw six wide fingers wrapped around the handle of his sword. The three soldiers stood at attention as the general rebuked them with his thundering voice. "The best of these Jewish scumbags are kindling for the cooking fires of our great Dagon! Yet you can't even subdue one frail little maiden? Where are the others?"

"We lost them."

The general aimed his sword at the tallest of the three soldiers. "You lost them?"

"That's what I said."

Without skipping a beat, the general swung his sword through the beard of the tallest Philistine soldier, slicing his hair off at the chin before the soldier even knew what happened. Anna gasped for fear as the man's hair floated to her feet like a greasy rag caught in a breeze. The other two soldiers took a step back, mortified by the general's fury, yet amazed at the swiftness of his vengeance. The soldier with a missing beard brought both hands up to inspect his naked chin.

"You shame Dagon! You shame your people, you fleck of a man!" The general pointed his sword at the embarrassed warrior. Then he aimed his sword at Anna. "Bring this whimpering rodent back to camp. We'll find out what she knows."

"I won't tell you anything, you monster!" Anna's lip trembled as she reproved the cruelty of the huge genetic mutant. "You slapped a girl! What kind of animal are you?"

"I'm a Philistine animal!" The huge hairy man leaned toward her and grinned widely, and Anna saw that he had several extra teeth sticking out of his gums.

She slowly stood to her feet, cradling her red face with her hands as her right eye and cheek began to swell.

"What do you want us to do, General?"

"One little field mouse will ruin your wheat stores, men. You cannot pity the mouse. This" – he pointed his sword at her again, causing her to squint from the reflection of the sun off of the long blade – "is a Jewish spy. The best poison tastes like candy, men. Don't let her big blue eyes and the sheen of her yellow hair confuse you."

"Don't worry." The soldier behind Anna was still pinching his nose to try and stop the bleeding from his nostrils.

"Take her to the holding cell at camp." The general dropped his sword back into its sheath. "Sooner or later, she'll break." Anna trembled for fear of whatever it was that the huge smelly man meant by that.

"Yes General."

"This is the day of our final attack. The conflict ends today."

* * * * *

When they realized they weren't being followed, Charity snuck back with James and Daniel to try to discover what she could about the men who captured Anna. She overheard some of the conversation before the soldiers left with her.

"Why do they think Anna's a Jewish spy?" James scratched his head, bewildered.

"Dagon's the idol of the Philistines," Charity recalled, "and that big guy called himself a 'Philistine animal'."

"I thought Philistines were only in Bible times?"

"That's right Daniel." Charity patted his hand. "Maybe we're in Bible times."

"There's a baseball team named the Phillies, I think." James pointed in the direction in which the soldiers took off with Anna in tow. "Maybe they're the kind of freaky baseball fans that wear costumes for games."

"Come on James!" Charity raised her voice in frustration at her younger brother. "Those guys aren't baseball fans."

"There's a steak sandwich named the Philly." Daniel licked his lips, fantasizing of dinner. "Maybe they're from an Ohio city that's famous for cookin' Philly sandw —"

"That's crazy. You're just sayin' that 'cause you're hungry."

"How'd you know I'm hungry?"

"Because you're *always* hungry!"

"Keep your voice down," said James as he gazed overhead at three huge squawking vultures that flew in circles above them. He squatted lower behind the wide tree. "So you think that we traveled back into Bible times in some kind of tornado?"

Charity took a deep breath. "It did happen in the Bible."

"Where?"

"After Philip baptized the Ethiopian eunuch in Acts, the Bible says he was whooshed over to some other place."

"Is 'whooshed' in the Bible?" wondered Daniel.

Doubt clouded James' features. "I don't know guys. Didn't they speak Hebrew or Philistinese or something like that in Bible times? How come those guys were speaking English?"

Charity looked overhead and squinted as she studied the circling vultures that had captured James' attention. "They did have a strange accent I never heard. Maybe they weren't really speaking English. Maybe we just *heard* them in English. What if whatever made us travel back in time also took care of the language differences so we could understand them?"

Daniel snapped his fingers. "The gun did it. We all touched that rusty musket at the same time when this happened, right?"

Charity nodded, deep in thought. "Remember, that gun turned into a slingshot when we got transported to this place. Why?"

"Maybe," Daniel proposed, "it's because they don't have guns in Bible times."

"Yeah, and God wants us to have a weapon that won't make us stand out." James took the slingshot out of his pocket, and studied it.

Charity shook her head at her younger brother's idea. "Slingshot or no slingshot, I think three reddish-blonde kids in a land of bearded brunettes makes us stand out. Look at our clothes anyway. I doubt they have shirts around here that have 'Old Navy' or 'Jesus Saves' written on them," she said pointing to James' T-shirt and then Daniel's.

"Whatever's happening to us, we still believe in God, right?" James swallowed his fear. He needed to stay strong for Daniel and Charity. "We need to trust Him and we need to find our sister. Now, those soldiers can't hide their tracks. I say we follow 'em, and try to find some goatskin outfits or something on the way to help us blend in."

"I ain't wearin' no goatskin," Daniel insisted with a shake of the head.

His bad grammar made Charity miss Anna terribly.

They traveled several hours through the woods toward some smoke that rose from fires along the horizon. The soldiers' trail disappeared in a well-trodden muddy road, and the children entered a small village of two dozen houses with narrow dirt roads. The sounds and smells of animals filled the air. There were goats and sheep herded into small pastures fenced with split logs. At first, they couldn't find any people. Further down the lane they saw why. The smoke wasn't coming from chimneys or bonfires. It was coming from a burning house.

Charity, James, and Daniel joined a line of people who were passing along buckets of water from the well toward the burning home. Charity stood next to another redheaded, freckle-faced boy about her age, and thought, *There are redheads here after all.*

"What happened here?" Charity took a bucket out of the hands of the lad with the head full of bushy hair and handed it down to James.

"The Philistines. They're always looting and burning homes and kidnapping people."

"Yeah, they kidnapped our sister Anna not far from here."

The boy shook his head and bit his lip. "I'm sorry."

"Can you help us find her?"

"Uh, maybe after I'm finished with this mission I'm on for my papa."

Once the fire was under control, the Johnstons chatted with the redheaded boy about the Philistine conflict as he headed back to his horse carriage.

Charity stroked the mane of the black and white paint mare strapped to the carriage. "Do you know where they could be keeping our sister?"

The boy shook his head as he hopped into the carriage. "Probably at their camp. There's a major battle brewing not far from here."

"Where are we anyway?"

"Elah. Elah in Judah."

"Hey!" Daniel called out to the young man when he got a glimpse of some round loaves of bread in the back of the carriage. "Can we have some of that bread?"

"My papa instructed me to take that food to my brothers. The battle line is on the other side of these hills. Maybe someone there can help us find your sister. Hop in."

James and Daniel sat on each side of the redheaded boy, while Charity sprawled out on top of the bags of parched corn in the carriage.

"Be careful not to squish the bread back there."

"I'll take any squished pieces." Daniel grabbed his growling stomach.

"Here you go." The redheaded Israelite took a slice of bread from the satchel at his feet and handed it to Daniel.

"Thanks." Daniel smiled and took a bite.

The redheaded boy clicked his tongue, ordering his horse to trot. "Where are you from?"

"I guess you could say that we're foreigners," James responded.

"Do you worship the God of Abraham, Isaac, and Jacob?"

"Absolutely." Daniel and James shared a grin and then slapped a high five.

"Praise the Lord!" Daniel exclaimed through a mouthful of bread.

James glanced back at Charity and winked. Charity knew they

were in Bible times now. But when and why? It was still all a mystery to her, like a strange dream from which she would soon awake.

The bushy-headed carriage driver grinned at the strange children's enthusiasm for God. "Selah."

"La!" James responded with a cheesy grin.

"Huh?"

"Never mind."

"My brothers went to defend the kingdom while I had to stay home to watch the sheep. At least I get to visit their camp. I really wish I could be there fighting with them, doing big things for God."

"If you're obeyin' your parents, then you're obeyin' God, and that ain't no small thing, James responded. "Like my parents always say, if you'll be faithful in the small things, then God will give you the opportunity to be faithful in the big things."

"Whoa!" The three boys simultaneously gasped as they turned the sharp corner around the mountain and the valley spread out before them.

"What's going on?" Charity poked her head up above the railings of the carriage to see what had so excited the three boys. On the left side of the valley in front of them were tens of thousands of warriors dressed just like the fellows who kidnapped Anna. On the right side of the valley were the Israelites, their shields reflecting the bright noon sun. The smell of smoke from the soldiers' campfires filled her nostrils.

"The battle line is closer than I thought. My brothers are definitely going to be clashing swords today. Yes!"

"A real live battle?" James glanced at Daniel. "Maybe we can help."

"Don't even think about it, James." Charity's critical tone caused James to look over his shoulder at his sister. "We need to find Anna and get home."

"Don't worry," said the redheaded Israelite. "I'll take you to someone who can help you find your sister." The young man looked over at James. "So you can fight, huh? You don't look a day over eight."

James smiled broadly, pointed to heaven, and quoted one of his favorite Bible verses: "He teaches my hands to war, so that a bow of steel is broken by my arms."

"Amen. I'll have to remember that."

"It's from Psalm 18."

"Maybe we could put it to music. I love to play. What instruments do you play?"

"The piano and the guitar."

"I can play 'What a Mighty God We Serve'." Daniel stretched out his left hand and acted as if were strumming a guitar with his right hand.

The Israelite smiled as he pulled the carriage to a stop in the rear of their camp. One of the boy's big brothers rushed right up to the carriage.

"We're here to get help finding Anna," Charity reminded her brothers, "not to sight-see."

"My big brother, Eliab, is an acquaintance of the King." The Israelite lad pointed at the tall man with the full beard who tossed two fifty-pound bags of parched corn over his shoulders. "If anyone can help you find your sister, he can."

Two other warriors joined Eliab unloading the carriage. Without even greeting his little brother, Eliab asked, "What else did you bring?"

"There's some cheese back there, too." The redheaded boy hopped down and started passing out the food to his brothers.

"I must speak to whoever's in charge." Charity planted herself in front of Eliab to force him to pay attention to her. "My sister's been kidnapped by the Philistines and we have to rescue her. We also learned top-secret information about their battle plans. They want to end the war today."

The eldest of the brothers massaged his beard as he listened to Charity boldly make her case. He mumbled something to one of his brothers and then turned back to Charity. "Come with me."

Charity motioned to Daniel and James, and ordered, "Stay within earshot of the carriage. Don't go far."

James grinned mischievously. "Hey, it's me! Am I the kind of person that would venture off to the front lines of a strange battle in Bible times?"

Charity sighed and shook her head. "Precisely."

Daniel and James made their way to a shallow creek beside the carriage in order to get a better view of the enemy soldiers across the valley. James scooped up some small shells and colorful rocks, and filled his pockets with his favorites.

The Israelite boy finished distributing food to his brothers and then came over to see James' collection of rocks.

"Check this out." James extended a shiny white rock out to him and the young lad studied it. "What's that noise?" They heard some loud shouting on the other side of the Israelite camp.

"Let's go see."

They joined several soldiers who foraged the shallow creek and climbed to the top of a small hill. From there, they could get a good view of the action and still keep their eyes on the carriage. They saw a huge Philistine standing in the bottom of the valley, mocking and taunting the Israelites.

"Whoa! He's huge!" Daniel couldn't believe his eyes.

When the monstrous mountain of muscle began to curse the God of the Israelites, James grew angry. "I can't believe he said that. Who does he think he is?" He reached down and picked up a stick about as long as his arm, and pointed it at the Philistine warrior and glanced over at the bushy-haired Israelite boy. "God's gonna whoop some tail today."

The Israelite appeared equally infuriated. He tapped a soldier beside him on the forearm. "Did that Philistine just say what I think he said?"

"Yep." The soldier was decked with armor, held a spear in one hand and a sword in the other, but they could sense anxiety in his tremulous voice. "He's daring one of us to fight him. If one of us beats him, they'll be our servants. If he beats one of us, then we must become the Philistines' servants."

"That sounds like a good deal." The Israelite boy smiled at the fear-stricken soldier. "You guys can be free with less bloodshed."

"Ha!" The soldier laughed mockingly. "Get a look at that guy! He must be ten feet tall and 500 pounds of pure muscle."

"Watch this." James swung his stick around his body and over his head with dizzying speed, and finished off his imaginary enemy with a front snap kick and a thrust of his imaginary sword. "I'm a green belt. And I've got a pretty mean front snap punch too."

The bushy-haired Israelite boy chuckled. "Are you color-blind? Your belt is brown, like mine." The young Israelite grabbed the belt around his waist.

"Wow, you're almost a black belt."

The Israelite boy's facial expressions contorted and he looked over at Daniel as if expecting him to interpret what his older brother meant. When Daniel didn't respond to the lad's confused grimace, the lad turned back to James. "I really don't know what you're talking about."

"You're not into karate, huh?"

"No, but I'll tell you what I am into. I'm into taking that giant up on his deal. If none of these experienced soldiers wanna do it, I suppose God'll have to use me."

"Why don't we do it together?" James suggested. "There's no reason why you should go out there by yourself."

"No, James." Daniel grabbed James by the shoulder. "This ain't make-believe. This is real live fighting to the death."

James swatted away Daniel's hand, spurning his caution. "Oh, it's nothin' for God."

The soldier with the brown beard had been standing there listening to this childish fantasizing, his patience being tested as these two boys were inadvertently insulting the experienced Israelite warriors all around them. The soldier finally protested, "That warrior you take so lightly, you little rascals, is the mightiest warrior in the Philistine army, which is the mightiest army in the world! He could rip you in half with his bare hands. Plus, he's got four brothers almost as big as he is right behind him. And they've got twelve toes and twelve fingers!"

"Aw, it'd be like David and Goliath," shouted James. "I can do all things through Christ who strengthens me."

The redheaded Israelite looked at him cross-eyed. "What did you just say?"

"I can do all things through Christ who strengthens me. If we trust in God, we'll beat 'em. And if not, we'll die trying and go to heaven, and it doesn't get any better than that." James stretched out his right hand and pointed in the general direction of the mammoth Philistine. "Behind 'Door number 1', victory over a mountain of pagan muscle." With his left hand, he pointed in the opposite direction. "Behind 'Door number 2', dying and going to heaven forever. Ah. It's like asking a starving man to choose between Oreo cookies and banana pudding."

"What's an Oreo cookie?" the redheaded Israelite and the soldier asked simultaneously.

James looked at them as if they had just said they were from outer space.

The redheaded Israelite caught James' incredulous glance and scratched his head. "I'm sorry, friend. You lost me somewhere around 'Door number 1'."

The soldier with the long brown beard interrupted the childish enthusiasm and said, "General Goliath is a warrior's warrior." He pointed at the giant man in the middle of the valley ahead of them, and then snarled at James: "Don't be a fool, boy!"

James was stunned. "His name is Goliath?" It all began to make sense to him. The Bible story flashed through his head like a movie in fast forward. "How many days has this guy done this? Come out and dared y'all to fight him like this?"

"Today makes forty days, I think."

James' eyes lit up. "Well, that means David's about to take him on. I can't believe I get to watch this. Yee ha!"

"Who?"

"David, the son of Jesse, the next King of Israel. He must be around here somewhere."

"How, how, uh, how'd you know *my* name?" the redheaded Israelite asked, bewildered at the words that were protruding from this strange boy's lips.

James jerked his head around and stared at the boy with the bushy red hair standing beside him. "You're David?"

Daniel smiled giddily and poked James in the ribs. "I can't believe this is happening."

James high-fived Daniel in a fit of ecstasy while little David and the Israelite soldier just watched the duo, confused.

Daniel was mesmerized at the sight of the fearless General Goliath gradually approaching the front line of the Israelite army, mocking them and daring someone to come out and fight him. The soldiers beside the three boys back-peddled away from the approaching Philistine general. Daniel squinted and thought he recognized the huge Philistine. His eyes brightened. He tapped James on the arm. "Hey! I can't believe it, but I think that's the same man that kidnapped Anna."

* * * * *

"Lots of children have been kidnapped." The king's guard shrugged his shoulders at Charity and then darted his eyes to Eliab, the eldest son of Jesse, who stood dutifully at attention outside of the king's tent. "We're at war. The king does not have time to entertain children's unrealistic rescue plans."

Charity stepped closer and swallowed hard, finding her mouth very dry right at that moment. "But, sir, my sister may be killed."

"All the more reason for us to let the king alone so that he can devise a plan to end this war as soon as possible." The man was as immovable as the lean features of his tanned face.

"She said she was an ambassador," Eliab informed the guard, wary lest the young woman's protest be taken too lightly.

"Ambassador of what?" The guard's tone informed them of his disbelief that this thin redheaded girl who couldn't be a day over twelve would be an ambassador of anything besides a children's tree fort.

"The United States of America, and, and," Charity stuttered until she finally blurted out, "and of King Jesus."

The guard crossed his arms over his chest. "Never heard of the Unites States of King Jesus before."

"Not the Unites States of King Jesus, sir, but—"

"Let me see a token of your kingdom."

"A token?"

"Yeah. Proof. I want to see proof that you're an ambassador."

"Here." She pulled her MP3 player out of her pocket and extended the headphones toward the guard. "Listen to this."

The guard stared at Charity with a confused look on his face without taking her headset. After a pause, the guard laughed. "I don't hear anything."

"You gotta put these little earbuds in your ears, silly. Just do it. You've never seen technology like this." The guard reluctantly put the headphones up to his ears and Charity pushed play.

Suddenly, the guard's eyes lit up like Christmas trees. "Unbelievable! What is that?"

"Amazing, isn't it?" Charity smiled as Eliab took one of the headphones and put it to his ear. They were amazed that a sound so full and exuberant could come through a little trinket like Charity's little purple MP3 player.

The guard pointed at the earpiece. "Who in the world is this?"

"That's my pastor, Aaron Bounds and the Anchor Church choir."

"What kind of instrument is that?"

"That's him playing the harmonica, and singin' 'There's Power in the Blood.' Impressive, huh?"

"Your pastor's in here?" The guard pointed at the purple MP3 player that Charity held in her hand as he hugged the earphone to his cheek.

"How can a man be that little?" Eliab wondered.

Charity laughed at their childish amazement.

The guard's eyes grew wide and a hopeful smile crept on his lean facial features. "Can we get them scheduled for the Feast of Weeks? The king would be so pleased!"

Charity grinned as she recalled the Feast of Weeks in the Old Testament, also known as the Feast of Pentecost. "Sorry." She pulled the earbuds out of their ears and put them back into her pocket. "They'll be singing at Pentecostal services soon enough, but I must speak to the king immediately."

* * * * *

"All I need is fifteen soldiers or so, King. Just fifteen soldiers, and we can create a diversion over here." Charity pointed to the map of the location of the Philistines' camp on the table. "With a disguise, I'll try to sneak into their camp and break her loose."

"I'm sorry, Miss Ambassador of the Unites States of King Jesus." The king, dressed in battle clothes, was entertained by the young lady's ambition and her country's impressive musical technology, but he thought this rescue plan was foolish. "We are going to battle today, and I cannot spare any men for your diversion."

"Please," Charity begged. "This is my sister!"

"King Saul!" James barged suddenly into the tent, followed by an anxious guard who was unable to stop the young boy as he zigzagged away from his grasp and burst into the king's presence uninvited.

"I'm sorry, King Saul." The guard trembled as he tried to catch the little pest who was about to cost him his job. Two soldiers rushed and pointed their spears at James' chest and he put his hands up in the air, giving the guard his opportunity to wrap his hands around the boy's throat.

"Please!" James coughed as the guard began to tighten his chokehold.

"That's my brother!" Charity protested. "Leave him alone."

"I must speak to King Saul!" James hollered between coughs. "It's a matter of life and death. The Messiah, the Messiah…"

One of the king's captains stepped forward and placed the tip of his sword in between James' lips, silencing him.

"Don't kill him, Jonathan," King Saul stopped his son. "Not yet." King Saul stepped forward and put his hand on his son's shoulders and stared into James' eyes. "Explain yourself, little man."

The guard lightened his grip around James' throat and Jonathan withdrew his sword about six inches. James took a deep breath.

"He's with me, King." Charity pulled the soldiers' spears away from her brother and Jonathan lowered his sword. "I'll explain, but James, did I hear you right? Did you say this was King Saul?"

"And this is King David – great, great, great, granddaddy of the Messiah." James pointed at the freckle-faced bushy-headed boy who poked his head into the door of the tent. "And the giant Philistine out there in the valley is Goliath, who is the same fellow that kidnapped Anna."

"*King* David!" King Saul was not pleased with this announcement. "That little lad's a king? King of what? Does he dare to threaten the reign of the house of Saul?" He glanced at his son Jonathan, who dutifully raised the point of the sword to James' throat.

Little David didn't know what to think of the accusation. "I am son of Jesse of the house of Judah, brother to Captain Eliab. I have no idea what he's talking about, King."

"No, um, he doesn't know what I'm talking about, King Saul." James was about to inadvertently turn little David into an enemy of King Saul. "But you have to trust me. David's very important to you, and to Israel."

David blushed at the flattering words of James, and was wondering if he were a prophet. No one but his immediate family knew that Samuel had anointed David to be king, and the prophet had insisted on strict secrecy. Now, this strange orange-headed boy named James stood before the King of Israel and announced it to everybody.

James could have kicked himself for letting the cat out of the bag like that. "There's no greater friend of your kingdom than David, son of Jesse. You must let him accept the challenge of that giant Philistine out there in the field. If you let him do it, *you* will win a great victory today."

* * * * *

Daniel remained outside the King's tent where he heard Eliab and his brothers complaining of how David was embarrassing them with this nonsense of taking on General Goliath.

Daniel stepped in the midst of them and gathered his boldness to reprove them. "Where's your faith, Eliab? Don't you know that God has given you the Promised Land?"

"Well, tell that to them." Eliab pointed in the direction of the Philistines.

"Tell it to God," another one of the brothers mumbled.

"It says in God's law why the wicked rule over you," Daniel ventured to bravely assert. "It's because of sin. You'd conquer the Promised Land if you'd trust God."

"You sound like little David, you arrogant little boy."

"Well, thanks for the compliment."

"We're going to take that little haughty baby brother of ours and we're going to have a servant tie him up and take him home in a burlap sack."

"You sound like Joseph's brothers just before they sold him into slavery, all because of envy. I'll not let you do it."

"Oh?" Eliab snickered at the little blonde boy's audacity to speak to warriors with such authority. He winked at the brother beside him. "Really? What are you going to do about it?"

Daniel put his right index finger right into the center of Eliab's chest armor. "Your little brother and I might not look like much, but we're just the kind of people God likes to use. Pure hearts, not big muscles, win big victories. Just because you don't have the faith to trust God for victory, doesn't mean you need to throw water on your brother's fire. You should consider yourself lucky to carry his shoes. In a thousand years, no one's even gonna know your name, but your little brother will be the most famous king in the whole world. Your grandkids will sing his songs and heaven's angels will cheer his courage."

* * * * *

"I can't fight with these." Little David wiggled uneasily in the heavy armor. "They don't fit."

King Saul appeared to take offense. "If you're going to represent me, you need my armor and weapons." If King Saul wasn't going to personally face the infamous Philistine general, he at least was going to have his armor and weapons represent him in the conflict.

Charity's eyes lit up. "James, give him the slingshot."

James nodded and reached into his pocket. "Oh yeah. Here. I almost forgot about this." He pulled the slingshot out of his pocket and held it out to David. "And here's a few stones." James reached into his other pocket and took some rocks from his collection of favorites.

"Ah." David took off the armor and reached for the slingshot. "Now this is a weapon I can wield with some accuracy. I've killed a lion and a bear with one of these. I'll need five stones. This one" - David held up a round, shiny white one - "is going to be impaled into that uncircumcised Philistine's brain over there. The other four are for his brothers if they butt in."

James and Charity looked at each other for a moment and smiled. James patted Daniel on the shoulder. "I just love this guy!"

When David and James left the tent, Charity stood before the king and continued to try to plead her case for her plan to rescue Anna. But the king appeared to have a blank look on his face, as if he wasn't paying attention to her.

"King Saul?" After a pause, Charity glanced at the captain beside the king.

The captain leaned over to make eye contact with his king. "What's the problem, King?"

King Saul took a deep breath. "I'm having second guesses about this little shepherd boy taking on Goliath. What was I thinking? If by some miracle that boy beats Goliath, then I'll look like a coward for not taking on that monster myself. If the boy fights him and is killed, I'll look like a fool for letting a boy fight a skilled military general."

Charity sympathized with King Saul in his dilemma. "I've got a suggestion. Why don't you offer a large reward to whoever kills Goliath? Why not offer your daughter's hand in marriage to the victor? That'll put your hand in the victory, make it look like your reward was the motive behind whoever volunteered."

The king smiled. "You have much wisdom and foresight, Miss Ambassador of the United States of King Jesus."

Charity grinned sheepishly and bowed low before the King. "I wish," she mumbled. "Like my grandmother says, we must 'think ahead to avoid danger.' And speaking of thinking ahead, I would like to have a word with your daughter Michel before she marries David. We've got to work on her love for dancing."

* * * * *

James, Daniel, and David made their way through the crowd of trembling Jewish soldiers to the front lines of battle.

"You're crazy!" Eliab shouted out to David as he walked past. Daniel could see that David was discouraged by his brother's lack of confidence in him.

"Don't listen to him, David" Daniel patted him on the shoulder. "You're not crazy - you're normal. They don't believe in God's power. They're the crazy ones. They're not going to have books of the Bible written about them. You are."

* * * * *

"No, I'm not marrying that pagan!" Anna refused to give in to the threats and persuasion of the smelliest and fattest of the pagan Philistine priests. Her hands were tied to the thick wooden pole in the midst of a cluttered tent as the priest attempted to persuade her of the remarkable opportunity she had to marry the son of a chief of generals in the Philistine army. "The Bible says to not be unequally yoked with unbelievers."

The priest grinned condescendingly. "He's handsome, he's strong, and he likes you."

"He's a pervert! By the length of his beard, he's got to be thirty – I'm only ten."

"He's rich, too."

"I don't care, I will *not* marry an idol-worshippin' Philistine who obviously doesn't brush his teeth and who smells like my baby sister's dirty diaper."

"You will!" The priest abandoned his attempts to persuade the stubborn slave girl and began to shout at her with his finger pointed in her face. "Or you will burn in the fires of our god Dagon!"

Anna was not intimidated. "That'll only last five minutes, but you're gonna burn in hellfire forever if you hurt me!"

"Oh, I am, huh?"

"You have no idea who my Father is!"

The priest beckoned the guard who stood at the tent's entrance. "No food or water for twenty-four hours." He gave Anna a sharp glance. "We'll see if your tongue's as sharp when it's as dry as the desert sands."

Anna raised her chin in defiance of her mistreatment, and tried to think heavenly thoughts.

When they left the tent, Anna's tears began to flow. She was beginning to feel pain from the slap in the face that the giant soldier gave her, and from the ropes tied tightly around her wrists. It was a miracle that they were here at all, but even Lazarus, who was raised from the dead, died again. Does God do His miracles for His glory and then let us drift the rest of our lives in a sea of chance and hope? Does God really care about our suffering and pain? In a world of billions of suffering people, would He really stoop from heaven's throne to answer her one little prayer? She was so small in the grand scheme of things, like a common toad in a zoo full of rare animals. Maybe she should just be thankful for salvation and not let her expectations be so high for God. She wasn't important enough to God to expect Him to do another miracle just for her.

Or was she? Did God love her like a king loves a single faceless pauper? Or did He really love her like a father loves his child?

A Scripture came to her mind: "He that spared not His own Son upon the tree, how shall He not freely give us all things?"

There it was – a promise, a life raft that she could cling to in the midst of this nightmarish storm. That Jesus died on the cross to save her from sin wasn't evidence that there was no miracle left for her. But rather, it was evidence that there was a bottomless pit of miracles available to her, if she only believed.

She raised her tear-filled eyes to heaven. "Father, I believe you are good. You are my only hope. I believe in You, help mine unbelief." Her tears transformed into a pitiful sob as she poured her heart out to God. "Please, God, please help them find me. Please!" She paused to gather her emotions as one would gather a pocketful of coins that had fallen to the ground. She would not beg from God, for that in itself is evidence of unbelief. The Father knows what she needs before she asks, and He loves her. Careless, repetitious begging in the midst of the storm of doubt and fear that whizzed around in her mind would not bring about her miracle, only an unshakeable, courageous faith in a miracle-working God. And faith is incompatible with fear. She would not be afraid. She would believe. "I know you will help them find me," she calmly prayed. "Thank you, my dear Father. Unless," she paused to add, "unless you can get more glory from my suffering. Then let your will be done."

The Father leaned forward in His throne and grinned with pleasure. "That's my girl."

* * * * *

"Yay! Whoohoo!" James and Daniel shouted with glee when David's stone struck Goliath right between the eyes. They had front row seats to one of the greatest battle scenes in the history of the world. The whole Israelite army began to stomp and clap and shout praise to God.

The Philistine stumbled and fell to the ground with a thunderous crash from his heavy metal armor.

"It's a miracle!" James shouted with his hands raised heavenward.

Daniel gave his big brother a hug. "Praise the Lord! God did it!"

David turned to face his friends, and with a huge smile on his face, he exclaimed, "I will call upon the Lord, who is worthy to be praised. So shall I be saved from my enemies!"

"He's waking up!" Daniel pointed to Goliath. "He's waking up! David! He's not dead yet!"

Everybody was too busy cheering and shouting to realize that the giant Philistine was beginning to move. Daniel saw him moving his arms, and was wondering if he was reaching for his sword. Daniel ran into the valley, screaming, "David! Kill him! Kill him!"

James was too busy high-fiving other soldiers to realize that Daniel had ventured into the valley. He turned and yelled, "Daniel! Get back here!"

David could not understand what Daniel was saying because of all of the singing and the shouting. He thought Daniel was running out there to give him a high-five. But Daniel banked right over to the fallen giant, picked up his gleaming wide sword, and handed it to David. "Cut his head off, quick!"

"What? Why? He's dead already." David was reluctant to take the sword.

"The guy's still moving. I saw him."

"You do it."

"It's in the Bible. You gotta do it."

"What? You mean the law of God?"

"God's book is still being written."

"What?"

"Yeah, the half has not been told. You've gotta do it." Daniel thrust the sword into his hands. "Do it!"

It was then that David first saw Goliath move a little. "You're right, he's still alive!"

Daniel clapped and cheered him on. "Get him right through the neck!"

David raised the sword over his head, looked over at Daniel with amazement, and smiled from ear to ear. He dropped the mighty sword down with a grunt and cut the head off with one swoop. Then he turned to face his countrymen to shout praise to God, bringing the Israelites to a frenzy again.

"Wait!" said Daniel. He reached down, removed Goliath's helmet, and picked up Goliath's huge head by the beard.

"Oh gross!" David remarked.

Daniel extended the head toward David. "Here, take this to King Saul. He'll love it."

"Yeah. That's a great idea." He reached for and took Goliath's head by the hair. Then he began to dance and jump up and down as he sang a spontaneous song of praise to the Lord. Daniel joined him, shouting praise to heaven as goose bumps covered his body.

When the Philistines finally realized that their champion had been defeated, they began to flee. Even the four brothers of Goliath took off. The warriors of Israel gave chase, and began to smite down the Philistines as they ran away.

* * * * *

As the Philistines fled, Charity, James, and Daniel ran with the Israelite soldiers into the Philistine camp. There was fighting all around them, but they had one thing on their mind: finding Anna.

"There she is!" James pointed at a fat man in a bright orange outfit who was shoving Anna and some other bound women onto the back of a horse-drawn carriage about thirty yards away.

The man jumped into the front seat of the carriage and began to crack a whip over the horses' heads.

"Oh no! We're going to lose her." Daniel began to sprint in the direction of the carriage, followed by Charity.

"No we're not." James bent down and picked up a fallen spear. He flung it as hard as he could at the front of the carriage. It went through the front wheel of the carriage and stuck into the ground, causing the spokes of the wooden wheel to splinter. The fat Philistine who drove the carriage was thrown over top of it and landed on the backs of one of the horses. He rolled off to the side and began to flee with a limp as the Israelite soldiers gave chase.

Charity was the first to make it to Anna and the other captive Israelite women. "You're going to be all right." Charity had tears of joy in her eyes as she embraced her sister.

Daniel cut Anna's wrist-ties with a pocketknife. "Praise the

Lord we found you."

"Thank God." Rivers flowed from Anna's big blue eyes and down her cheeks. "That's some mighty good spear-throwing, James."

"Thanks."

Charity looked closely at Anna's eye. "Your eye's turning all black and blue. What happened?"

"I'd say it looks pretty good given that I've been slapped in the face by Goliath," she said with a chuckle.

"Awesome!" Daniel held his palm in the air and his sister slapped him a high-five.

"I'll never wash my face again." Anna's spontaneous humor made them all laugh.

Charity wiped Anna's tears and grasped her hands. "You're not going to believe what has happened today."

Anna sighed. "Let's just get out of here. I want to go home so bad."

Daniel cut the last wrist-tie of the captive women and walked up to Charity and Anna. "How are we going to get home?"

James turned to Daniel. "You know, we touched Johnny's musket all at the same time to get here and then it turned into that slingshot. So maybe we should all touch the slingshot at the same time to go home."

Charity nodded. "Let's go find David and get that slingshot back."

"Wait a minute." James paused. "I'm tempted to stay. Maybe Daniel and I could be two of David's mighty men." Daniel winced, and turned to Charity, who was aghast at James' proposal.

"You're crazy, James!" She put her hands on her hips. "We gotta go home. Aren't you gonna miss Mom and Dad?"

"Yeah," Anna chimed in, "and Grace, Elijah, and little 'Baitee'?" ("Baitee" was the nickname for their youngest sibling, one-year-old Faith. They called her "Baitee" because that's how the three-year-old Elijah pronounced her name.)

James smiled warmly at the thought of his baby sister. "I guess you're right."

Anna massaged her wrists, blistered from the tight ropes that bound her all day. They walked toward the Israelite camp in the light of a setting sun. When they arrived, the spirit of celebration filled the camp. As they walked through the tents toward the king's chambers, James announced the cause of Anna's injury to everyone they passed, and the soldiers and servants heaped praise on her. They finally found David in Jonathan's tent, sitting and chatting excitedly with King Saul.

James and Daniel gave the bushy-headed Israelite boy a hug, congratulated him again, and then asked for the slingshot back.

He pointed to Jonathan, who was holding it and showing it to some of his friends. James, Daniel, and David walked up to him, and James tapped him on the shoulder. "Would you mind if I have my slingshot back?"

Jonathan nodded and handed it to him. "Sorry I stuck my sword in your mouth. I thought you were an enemy."

James smacked him playfully on the shoulder. "Just be glad I didn't groin-kick ya." James leaned close to Jonathan and whispered into his ear. "Good job with your armor-bearer against the Philistines in chapter 14. It's one of my favorite chapters in the Bible."

Jonathan's face revealed his confusion. "Huh? Chapter in what?"

"Never mind. Keep up the good work." He put a hand on David's shoulder and Jonathan's shoulder, and said, "Y'all stay close. You're going to need each other in the days ahead."

David gave James another hug. "Thanks for letting me borrow your sling, buddy. Couldn't have done it without you."

Across the room, Charity and King Saul were exchanging farewells. "Thank you for your counsel, Miss Ambassador to the United States of King Jesus."

"No, the United States *and* King Jesus."

"Huh?"

"Never mind. You're so welcome, King Saul. Oh, and if you are ever tempted to try and hurt David, like, throw a spear at him or anything like that, don't do it. You'll make God really angry if you do, okay?"

King Saul looked confused. "I'll try to keep that in mind."

* * * * *

They stepped outside the tent and Charity sighed deeply. "I can't believe God let us play a part in this."

They were amazed at how bright the stars looked in the skies of ancient Israel. James pointed upward. "There's Orion! Wow. God's a wonder, ain't He?"

"Isn't He," Anna corrected him, prompting them all to laugh and hug Anna one more time.

James held out the slingshot in his palm. "Let's go home."

One at a time, they each put a hand against the slingshot in James' palm, and suddenly the dirt around them on the desert ground was sucked into the air and began to swirl, forming a brown haze in all directions. They were in the whirlwind again.

Anna spoke her thoughts out loud. "Ah, that feels better."

"What?" Charity wondered.

"My eye."

James studied Anna closer and realized that her swollen, bruised eye was completely healed.

"Wow. It's as if it never happened."

Momentarily, the swirling brown haze above their heads began to slow and clear.

Chapter 3

T he Johnston children expected to find themselves in the woods behind their home, but as the mysterious swirling fog gradually lifted around them, they discovered that their adventure was far from over. They found themselves in front of a high stone wall as swarms of horror-struck, panic-stricken people ran past them into a small door beside a huge gate. Through the clutter of bustling people, they saw a long line of soldiers marching toward them. Many of the soldiers were on horseback, scurrying their war horses on the outskirts of the crowd, wielding bloody swords at the townsfolk who fled before them. The children's hair stood on end and their breath seemed to be snatched away as they observed the fear of those who fled the violence of the soldiers. Other soldiers on foot gathered the weary, the wounded, and the injured, and bound their hands. On the horizon beyond them were large wooden towers on wheels that were being pushed slowly toward them by slaves.

"The Romans found us!" a man with a bloody gash on his head screamed as he fled past them through the door. "Open the gate!"

"The guards won't open the gate!" someone in front of him responded. "We've got to enter through the door…"

Charity looked down and in her hands she saw a 14-inch double-edged dagger in an elaborate golden sheath. "What? Where's the slingshot?" She pulled on the handle of the weapon and was amazed at the strange engravings on the double-edged blade, and the elaborate golden handle. She resheathed the dagger and placed it inside the elastic of her skirt. Grabbing James and Daniel by the shoulders, she shouted, "Come on!" She turned them and pushed them in front of her toward the walled city. "Through the door! Hurry!"

Anna was as confused as she was terrified by the fear on the faces of all those around her. Both the men and women wore long robes, and the women had their heads covered. They all appeared frighteningly thin and haggard. Anna followed her siblings into the throng of people who pressed themselves through the small door beside the huge gate.

A little boy about Anna's age was weeping beside her. They were shoulder to shoulder in the dense crowd. "It's all right," said Anna, trying to comfort him. "We'll make it."

"It's not all right! They've got my sister!"

Anna turned around to see the tanned, muscular soldiers, with golden helmets decorated with red bristles that proceeded from the top of their helmets. Their horses inched closer as the soldiers continued threatening those who fled before them.

"Come on! Hurry! Hurry!" Charity pushed James and Daniel in front of her as they pressed toward the small door.

The people were in such a panic that three or four found themselves pressing through the small opening all at once, and they could not enter. "One at a time!" Charity urged them. Finally, someone on the inside of the walled city began to grab people's arms and pull them through the opening.

When Charity and her brothers finally pushed through the ancient stone entrance beside the huge wooden gate, she turned to see the guards in the city begin to close the small door. Charity stopped them, frantic that Anna was being shut outside the city. "No! My sister!" She put her foot in the door and prevented them from closing it.

"Move!" one of them ordered her, trying to push her away. "The Romans will enter if we don't bolt the door!"

Charity thrust her hand through the opening and Anna grabbed it. "No! My sister!"

"Let us in!" Anna begged, her voice dwarfed by a hundred people who struggled to enter the city all at once. "Please!"

One of the Jewish guards raised his sword and acted as if he was going to sever Charity's arm. "No!" Charity screamed, her eyes welling with tears. "She's right there!"

The crowd of panicking people who pressed against the door

forced it open even more. Anna poked her head through the door. "Wait! The boy!" To Charity's horror, she disappeared back into the mass of people outside the door.

"What are you doing? Anna!" Charity screamed, her voice barely audible over the roar of voices.

Momentarily, Anna pressed the small nine-year-old boy through the city door. She followed closely behind him and the door was finally shut. Anna and Charity turned in pity when they heard the throng of townspeople outside the door scream and bang on the door, begging to be let inside.

The guards inside breathed a sigh of relief as they barred the doors.

"Why won't you let them in?" Charity asked. "They're killing people out there."

"We're doing our job to keep you alive," one of the guards responded, objecting to Charity's insinuation. "You get!"

"Where are we?" Anna wondered between deep breaths of air. The stench of unwashed people all around caused her to put the sleeve of her shirt over her nose.

Charity, gasping with adrenaline, shrugged.

Anna bent to tend to the grieving boy beside her, who stared longingly at the bolted door. "They'll kill her!" he cried. "They'll crucify her!"

"Who?"

Without answering, the boy began to plead with the guards beside the door. "They got my sister! I have to go save her."

"Son, this locked door is saving your life. The Romans found you. You should have been more discreet."

The boy grabbed one of the guard's arms and the guard pushed him away.

Anna asked the fretful boy, "Did you say they're going to crucify your sister?"

"We came into the city against our parents' explicit instructions, to try to bring some food to our friends. But now the Romans have laid a terrible siege against this city and we're stuck here, starving. We were helping our friends try to scavenge food outside of the city walls when the Romans found us." The crowds around them began to thin as the people departed to their homes inside the city. "I'm not supposed to be here." He wiped his tears and took a deep breath. "I need to get my sister and find my parents!"

Charity and Anna tried to comfort the boy, who was about the same age as Anna.

Sympathizing with the young man, a white-bearded man in a long purple robe, decorated with white trim, bent low and tried to comfort him. "Put your trust in God, Johannine, the Messiah will come to save us."

"You've been saying that ever since I was born, Ananus."

"He will. Trust in Him! Remember what happened during the days of Hezekiah and Caligula just 30 years ago..."

"Wait!" Charity stopped the elderly man. "Where are we?"

The tall, white-bearded man studied Charity and Anna for a moment, puzzled at their unusual dress. He crossed his arms over his chest, leaned back, grunted, and rocked for a moment.

Charity found his rocking motion most unusual. "What is it?"

The man clenched his hands together and leaned down to get a closer look at the strange young, redheaded girl. "Are you trying to tell me that you don't know where you are?"

"We really don't know," Anna responded humbly.

"Jerusalem," the boy answered.

"When?"

"The tenth day of the month of Av."

"Av?" Anna had an inquisitive look on her face. "What year is it?"

Charity whispered into Anna's ear. "They don't tell time like we do." Charity turned to the white-bearded man. "How many years since Jesus died?"

"Jesus?" The white-bearded man balked and turned his attention to some commotion in the square beside them. "There are a lot of people named Jesus in Jerusalem."

"Jesus of Nazareth. You know, son of Mary and Joseph, born in a manger, crucified under Pontius Pilate and resurrected on the third..."

The young man's eyes lit up. "You believe in Jesus of Nazareth?"

Charity and Anna looked at each other, their eyes wide. "Of course!" Charity answered.

"It's been 37 years since Jesus' resurrection. My parents saw

Him before He ascended. They believe He was the Messiah…"

Without warning, the white-bearded man raised his hand and swung the back of it against the boy's face. "How dare you!" the old man exclaimed.

The boy raised both hands to cradle his bruised jaw. He shrunk away from the old man, preparing for another blow. Charity stepped between them. "What'd you do that for?"

"I am Ananus, the priest of the temple of the most High God; well, a retired priest anyway. And it is within my authority to stamp out the Christian abomination, especially among former pupils!" The old man stuck an arthritic index finger to within three inches of the young lad's frightened face. "Don't forsake the faith of your fathers, boy, or you'll get the skin scraped off your back by the temple whips, you hear me?" The old man turned to the commotion in the court-yard near them. "And there's another one of those abominations right now!" He turned and marched away from the three children and called out to two Levites who served as his guards. They were sitting in an alley drinking sips of wine from a leather bottle. "Sons of Levi! I told you to monitor this courtyard for fanatics!" They leapt to their feet, apologetic, and followed him through the crowd.

It was then that Charity and Anna realized that James and Daniel were missing.

"Where'd they go?" Charity and Anna began to scurry about, weaving in and out of the people of Jerusalem, who looked pale and strikingly thin. "James! Daniel!"

Johannine clung to Anna's arm, asking her questions rapidly, one after another, "Who are you? How come I've never seen you at church? How did you become a Christian? Where are your parents? Why did you come back to Jerusalem?"

"It's a long story, Johannine," said Anna as she followed Charity through the crowd, intermittently calling their brothers' names. "What do you mean, come back to Jerusalem?"

"Don't you know that all the Christians left?"

Anna stared into his brown eyes, bewildered. "Why?"

"Jesus told us to. He said that when you see the city surrounded by armies, flee for the mountains for the desolation of the city is at hand. Didn't you know that? Most of the Christians are residing at Pella in the mountains of Perea, a rock fortress hidden in hill country about sixty miles northeast of here."

"How did you flee the city if you were surrounded?"

"Not long ago, the Roman governor of Syria, Cestius Gallus, was leading the 12th Roman legion against the city and fought his way through the wall and into the city…"

"He made it inside?"

"Yes. But for some reason, when he got to the temple he unexpectedly retreated. The Jews counter-attacked and slaughtered the 12th legion."

"No way! Praise God!"

"Not so fast. The Jews took that victory as a sign that their independence was at hand, so they began a full-scale war. Then Christians left, just like Jesus told us to."

"But you pushed back the Romans. I don't understand."

"It was only temporary. The Romans soon returned under Titus, the son of the emperor, with plans for bloody vengeance. That's why Jesus told the Christians to leave, because He wanted to protect us. He knew that the Romans would return and destroy this city. Now the Romans have surrounded Jerusalem. People are starving to death, and there's even cannibalism."

"Yuck!" Anna stuck out her tongue and squinted her facial features.

"That's why we risked capture to sneak past the city gates at night to scavenge for food…"

"There you are!" Charity found James and Daniel at the front of a crowd of people before a man in a white robe with long brown hair. The tall, handsome man stood on the steps of a home that clearly belonged to a wealthy family, with wide white pillars that held up a second floor balcony.

"Hey! Come over here!" James waved them over. "Listen to this guy!"

"Don't you ever leave us again," Charity scolded him.

"You left us," Daniel responded. "We were getting pushed from behind…"

"Shh," Anna said, her eyes fastened on the tall preacher in the white robe. "Maybe he's one of the apostles."

"That man is not a Christian," Johannine said.

Anna placed her index finger over her lips. "Shh."

Three people knelt before the tall street preacher with the long brown hair. James looked over his shoulder and whispered to Charity, "Are we in the time of Jesus? Is that Jesus?"

"That's silly," Johannine responded. "He's a false prophet."

The preacher bellowed, "God spoke to me and told me to speak to the wall, and say, 'Thou shalt not fall!'" He stretched his arms before the great wooden gate as the people began to applaud his comforting words.

"I just saw him heal that lady on her knees from some kind of vision problem," said James as he pointed at one of the ladies in front of the stairs.

"She's worshiping him," Charity noted. "A Christian would never allow that."

"I am the Messiah!" the man in the white robe bellowed. "Hearken unto me! I am the one of whom Moses spoke, 'I will raise them up a Prophet from among their brethren, and will put My words in his mouth; and he shall speak unto them all that I shall command him'." The people stood in astonishment at the man's proclamation, hoping his words to be true.

"Nope," said James, shaking his head. "This definitely ain't a good guy."

"The Lord said," the preacher continued, "that whosoever will not hearken unto My words which he shall speak in My name, I will require it of him…"

Ananus the white-bearded priest ascended the stairs with the two sword-carrying Levites in tow. He planted himself beside the preacher. "That is blasphemy!" Two of the preacher's followers unsheathed their swords and rushed to stand between their preacher and the two armed Levites.

"This is outrageous!" Ananus shouted to the people. The preacher took a step back, taking shelter behind his armed followers. "The Messiah will deliver us from the Romans! What has this man done, besides ask us to violate the first commandment?"

"He healed me!" the woman on her knees shrieked, tears filling her eyes.

"If one splinter of wood from this gate or one pebble of rock from those walls falls," the preacher shouted authoritatively as he pointed at the large wooden gate in front of him with both hands, "then I am *not* the chosen one. Take heed: all who reject my words shall receive to themselves damnation! I am the King of the Jews, believe in me and you shall be delivered. For a small sum, I shall prophesy your future..."

Many Jews fell to their knees before the man and began to trust him to deliver them. Some extended silver coins toward him, asking him to prophesy blessing over them. The self-proclaimed prophet stuck his chest out and smiled as his followers pushed the armed Levites and the feisty old priest down the stairs.

Ananus turned and begged the Jews who made up the crowd, "Don't believe this imposter! You're the people of God, don't forget the commandments..."

The Levites feared for the priest's life, and so they began to urge him to retreat for the safety of an alley. Crowds parted to let them pass.

Momentarily, a huge pounding of the gate commenced, shaking the chains that strung the length and breadth of the huge wooden gate. With the first loud bang, part of the cement fortification that held the joints of the gate crumbled, falling to the ground.

"Ha!" Ananus bellowed as he turned to the prophet. "Some prophet you are!"

Everyone turned their attention to several Jewish guards who were atop the city wall beside the gate. "They're attacking with a battering ram!" one of them shouted. Another guard sounded the trumpet to call the archers to that part of the city wall. The men on top of the wall began to rain down arrows upon the Romans as the huge battering ram, made of logs and pushed by slaves, was thrust against the wooden gate over and over again.

"That man is a false prophet!" Ananus insisted before the crowd. The long-haired prophet in the white robe had a confused look on his face, almost as if he expected his prophecy to be true and was surprised when the rocks in the wall began to crumble and fall to the ground with the pounding.

"Ananus is right!" James bellowed. James confidently stepped to the foot of the stairs and turned to the people. "This man is a false prophet," he shouted, pointing at the man in the white robe. Another loud bang on the gate made the ground beneath their feet shake, and the people trembled for fear. "That passage that the false prophet quoted from Deuteronomy referred to Jesus Christ. Jesus is the only Messiah, and the King of the Jews!"

At hearing this, those who knelt at the front of the crowd jumped to their feet, instantly enraged at James. Accustomed to the freedom to evangelize in his country, James seemed astounded at their violent reaction. He took one more step up the stairs and bellowed, "Have I become your enemy because I tell you the truth?"

"James! No!" Charity said, motioning for him to step off the stairs. Several in the mob rushed James, trying to grab his hands. Charity reached for the dagger that she had put inside the elastic of her skirt, and only felt the sheath. "Oh no, where did it go?"

"What?" Daniel asked.

"The dagger's gone."

All at once, the mob descended upon James.

"Daniel! Charity! Help!" James reached for his siblings, but the crowd pressed tightly around him, blocking them from being able to see him. They raised their fists in the air, and cried out for the blasphemer to be punished. Charity squeezed between some people to try to free him from their grasp, but the mob was energized with fury. "Take him to the pole!" one of them screamed. The mob began to drag James down an alley.

"Oh no, the pole," Johannine mourned.

Charity's fearful gaze turned to their nine-year-old Christian Jewish friend. "What's the pole?"

The boy's face turned white. "They are taking him to the pole outside the temple. They are going to flog him."

"The pole outside the temple? You mean the temple, the real temple?" The boy nodded and Charity's eyes opened wide in amazement.

"Oh, that boy is so impulsive!" Anna opined.

"At least he's impulsive in a good way," Charity responded. "Let's follow, we've got to help him."

"How?" said Daniel, wiping his tearful eyes with the back of his hands. "Oh God, help James."

They pressed into the midst of the mob and tried to follow.

"There will be no divine help for us," mourned little Johannine. "We should have stayed away from Jerusalem. My parents warned me. Jesus foretold this would happen."

The events began to register in Charity's mind. She licked her lips, recalling the words of Christ. "The Romans will conquer the city. They will defile the temple..."

"The temple is already defiled, girl." This was the voice of Ananus, the retired priest. He was pushed by the mob in the same direction as the Johnstons and young Johannine. "I tried to persuade the people to rise up against the Zealots. With the help of the cruel Idumeans, those beasts slew 8,000 fellow Jews in the temple. 8,000!" He shook his head in disbelief. "Gentile enemies from without, and Jewish enemies from within. I barely escaped the Zealots' wrath. It would have been far better for me to have died before I had seen the house of God laden with such abominations and its unapproachable and hollowed places crowded with the feet of murderers." He turned to Charity. "Don't go to the temple. Your brother will probably recover. Just pray that the Messiah will deliver us before the Romans nail us to trees outside the city."

"There aren't any trees out there!" Johannine responded. "They've cut all of them down for crosses and for their siege towers."

They passed a house where several men were raiding an elderly woman's food stores. She screamed as one of them pinned her to the wall and dozens of others stuffed her dwindling supply of flour and dried fruits into satchels. "No!" she screamed from her front porch. "That's all the food I have! Please!"

Charity tried to stop to help the woman, but she saw that the thieves were armed with swords, and one of them was guarding the front porch. The crowd continued to push her down the alley. "Somebody help her! Why won't someone help this woman?"

A Jewish woman beside her answered, "Those are Simon Bar Gioras' men. They used to be with the Zealots, but now they're just a bunch of greedy looters."

Daniel, fearful for the woman's safety, turned to Ananus. "Can you help her?"

The priest Ananus shook his head and disappeared down a side alley. The mob continued to push them down the narrow sidewalk.

Anna turned to Johannine. "What do you mean that they don't have any trees outside of the city wall?"

"They've been crucifying five hundred people a day for weeks – anyone they find outside the city walls. The famine is making people desperate to leave to find food." Johannine leaned closer to the three Johnstons. "Give up hope of saving your brother. All grace has left Jerusalem, and judgment has come." Tears came to the boy's eyes. "If only my sister and I had stayed outside the city…"

Charity's confidence rebounded. "Johannine, God will never forsake you. He will never leave you. Don't despair…"

"Jesus warned us. We don't deserve His help." His tears swam down his face in rivers, making Charity's voice choke with emotion. "Now I'll never see my family again."

"Don't lose your faith in God. God hears our prayers and He loves us. Don't despair, Johannine. We'll do the best we can to protect you. But I have to find my dagger."

"What is it with this dagger you keep talking about?" Daniel asked.

"The slingshot turned into a dagger about this long" – she held her hands about 14 inches apart. "It had a golden handle. We needed to all touch the slingshot at the same time to get here, remember? Well, maybe we have to all touch the dagger at the same time to go home."

The pressure of the throng around them eased as the alley spilled into a courtyard. They slowed and stared in awe at the front gate of the temple. But their awe turned to horror when they saw that James' shirt had been ripped off and his hands were tied around a post as wide as a telephone pole. The rope that bound his hands was hooked to a nail on the other side of the pole.

"Are you saying that we are not God's special people, boy?" a Levite said as he snapped his whip on the ground behind James.

"Special to God? You're about to beat a child of God for speaking the Gospel truth. What do you think?"

The high priest stood beside the Levite with the whip. He wore a tall white cloth hat and an ephod, which was a vest encased with jewels and decorated with gold. He strutted slowly up to James. "We are the children of Abraham, Isaac, and Jacob! Are you saying that the Jews aren't God's chosen people?"

"God can of these stones raise up children unto Abraham," he cited Jesus' words from memory. "Can he turn your heart of stone into a heart of purity and tenderness? That is the question. He can, but only if you let Him."

"We are the chosen ones, the children of the promise by virtue of our heritage."

"You have been greatly blessed by God, no doubt. What other nation has been given the commandments on Mt. Sinai as you have? You were delivered from Egypt with a mighty hand." The priest's ego was coaxed by James' words, and he smiled broadly. "But I've read the curses too, at the end of Deuteronomy – you've read them." The high priest's smile disappeared, and he nodded soberly. "Then you know that the blessings of the covenant, like the curses, are conditional. Jesus told the unbelieving Jews in John chapter 8, you're of your father the devil, and the lust of your father you will do. Jesus is the Messiah prophesied by Isaiah in chapter 53, slain for the sins of the people. He is the way, the truth, and the life, and no man comes to the Father but through Him. Lord willing, your posterity will return to the Lord and be blessed, but only through Jesus."

With those courageous words, the rage of the crowd peaked and the man with the leather whip prepared to swing it against the lad's tender flesh. The priest's face turned red and he prepared to respond, but when he saw the tormenter prepare his leather whip, he quickly stepped aside to avoid getting struck.

"Please!" Charity rushed to the front of the crowd and put up both of her hands to stop the man with the whip. Amazed by her courage, he lowered his whip and let her speak. "Please, that's my brother, and we're not supposed to be here. Please have pity on him and let him go."

The high priest walked to Charity, the adrenaline-filled veins bulging out of his bony forehead. "Jesus was crucified because He was a false prophet..."

"Jesus prophesied this!" James responded. "He said that judgment was coming to this city and your people because you knew not the time of your visitation."

The man with the whip began to crack it on the ground beside James to drive fear into his heart. James shut his mouth, thinking that he had said too much, worrying that he had cast his pearls before swine like Jesus warned His followers not to do. He broke out in a cold sweat as he prepared his tender flesh for the thrash. "Help me be strong for you, dear God," he mumbled.

Just as the persecutor began to thrash his whip against James, an arrow pierced the air and struck him in the shoulder. He dropped the whip and fell to the ground. Several arrows began to fly all around them from inside the temple. Dozens of men rushed out of the temple with bows and arrows, firing indiscriminately into the crowd. Charity, Anna, and Daniel ducked but did not flee, not wanting to leave James. "The Zealots!" Johannine said, pulling on Charity's arm.

When the men with the bows ran out of arrows and unsheathed their swords, the three Johnstons ran for the cover of a nearby fountain. Once the Zealots had pushed back the crowd, their leader marched to James and cut his bonds with the tip of his bloody sword. "You're a brave young man who speaks of the Messiah. We need young men like you."

James swallowed hard, not sure if these men were trustworthy. He rubbed the rope burns on his wrists, and put his ripped shirt back on. "Thank you for coming to my rescue." He glanced around for his siblings, who had disappeared in the scuffle. He was glad to see that his brother and his sisters were not one of the ones who lay on the ground, writhing with arrows stuck in them. "Who are you, sir?"

"John of Gischala, the leader of the Zealots, Yahweh's faithful remnant. And you are?"

"James is my name." They shook hands and the cry of a young boy beside them got James' attention. The boy, who couldn't be a day over six, lay grabbing his foot, which was pinned to the ground with an arrow. One of John's men went and acted like he was going to run him through with his sword. James intervened and shouted, "Stop that!" He stood between the Zealot and the boy. "What do you think you are doing? He's not a threat to anybody."

"I told you, sir, this whippersnapper's not one of us!" the black-bearded Zealot howled. He pointed his sword at his leader, and then aimed it at James. "He'll defile us. Let's be rid of him!"

"Stay that sword," John of Gischala ordered as he walked up to the redheaded boy, massaging his long black beard.

Behind James, the brothers of the six-year-old had picked him up and were taking him to safety. "Thank you," one of them said as they headed down the road.

John of Gischala knelt down to get eye level with James. He put a hand on his shoulder. "James, did children perish when Saul slew the Amalekites?" James paused to try to recall the story and the man leaned closer to him. "If I recall, Saul lost his kingship because he didn't kill enough of them."

James nodded. "I suppose so, but..." James was distracted as the pounding of the Roman battering rams grew louder by the gate. He heard chunks of concrete begin to crumble inside the walls and crash to the ground.

"Enough small talk," the man said, patting James on the shoulder and standing to his feet. "Step inside the temple, and we'll talk about how you're going to help with our defenses." They began to walk toward the temple together. "You see, the Romans cannot fit into small places like you and other young brave defenders of Israel. So you can slip through a crack in the wall, strike, and retreat without leading the Romans back to us. You're valuable."

James liked the sound of that. "Really? I'm valuable?"

John of Gischala smiled. "More than you know." With his arm over James' shoulders, they walked past several other young men, carrying swords and spears, in the doorway of the temple. When they stepped through the outer wall into the courtyard, James gasped in awe. "The temple!" He stared in amazement at the bronze laver where the priests washed, and the altar where burnt offerings were made. They continued walking toward the stone porch that led to the Holy of Holies. "I can't believe it. It's the temple!"

"Yes. It never gets old, does it?" He paused to study James for a moment. "You look as if you've never seen it before."

James realized that this John of Gischala presumed him to be a Jew. He must not have been close enough to hear everything that James had said when he was being interrogated by the high priest. James shook his head and grunted, as if awaking himself out of a stupor. "What am I doing? I've got to get back to my sisters. They must be..." James stopped mid-sentence when he glanced beyond the thin layer of Zealots who stood armed against the wall. What he saw absolutely horrified him. Hundreds of dead bodies were piled up on top of each other like firewood against the wall of the courtyard.

He pointed, stunned. "What happened?"

John of Gischala did not even look at what James was pointing to. "God can be pushed to wrath, my friend. Sometimes, He delegates His remnant to do His work."

With the experience in the valley of Elah and the slaughter of the Philistines fresh in his mind, James nodded vigorously.

"We Zealots are ushering in the kingdom. Soon after splitting the Red Sea, God opened up the ground and swallowed Korah and his family down into the fiery pit. The Levites slew 3,000 when the law was given on Mt. Sinai. Must we expect less violence in the latter day glory than what we saw when the glory first descended?"

"There are children!" James said, pointing at some of the dead bodies. "Women!" The Zealots around him shifted their stances, doubting the wisdom of bringing this young child into their company, regardless of his appearance of bravery in the hands of the mob.

John of Gischala blushed at James' critical tone. He looked at the men around him and chuckled. "You've got a lot to learn, James."

"Apparently, you've got a lot to learn too. A dead body defiles the temple – you know that."

"In times of crisis, even David ate the shewbread. These people," the Zealot leader said as he motioned at the piles of dead bodies, "had the audacity to resist us, and in so doing they resisted God." He stuck his thumbs in his chest. "We are the Jews who are zealous for God's kingdom. We know that our people's spiritual whoredom is what postpones the coming of the Messiah and brings the Romans against us. Like Phinehas, we must thrust the javelin to turn the tide and make way for the blessing. We must prepare the way for the Messiah. God has called us to hold this temple as a garrison and a stronghold…"

James comprehended the comparison, but couldn't make sense of all the violence and confusion. Their conversation was backdropped by the Romans' war machine beginning to pound the city gate.

John placed a heavy hand on James' shoulder. "Judah," he called out to a nearby guard, "show James here how we demote fellow soldiers who criticize God's leaders. Get him digging with the other new recruits."

"Yes sir."

* * * * *

Charity, Anna, and Daniel were at a loss for what to do. The Roman war machines continued to threaten the gate of Jerusalem behind them, which some predicted would not last the day. The Zealots were destroying the Jews in front of them, violently occupying the temple. And the common men and women hated Christians so much that they tortured believers publicly until they recanted their faith. With so many Christians having fled the city, it seemed like any vestige of goodness had abandoned Jerusalem for the barrenness of the mountains.

Daniel's tears were flowing again. "I'm hungry," he complained.

"Tell me about it," Johannine interjected. "I haven't eaten a bite in six days besides some worms we found under a fallen log when we were scavenging for food outside the city walls."

"This is a horrible, horrible place," Daniel wept. "There are no good guys. Why did God bring us here?"

"Where the hand of God guides..." Charity paused and glanced at Daniel to let him complete the sentence.

"The hand of God provides," he responded, finishing the quote from their pastor.

"Let's trust in God," said Charity with a confident smile that soothed Daniel's fears.

"We can't just stay here, hiding behind this fountain," said Anna, as the Jews drew closer to the yard in front of the temple to grieve their lost loved ones. "Let's trust God some place safer."

"Follow me." Charity leapt to her feet with Anna right on her tail.

"Where are you going?"

"We gotta find that dagger, or we're not going anywhere." Daniel and Johannine ran as fast as they could to try to catch up. They ran past a mob of people who gathered around another one of their prophets. The leader stirred his followers into a frenzy, trying to motivate them to defend their city in spite of their growling stomachs and the fact that they were outnumbered three to one. "We will win this battle," the leader prophesied, "and you will eat the Roman soldiers' dinner before nightfall!"

The Johnston children ran with Johannine to the gate and ascended some narrow stone stairs that were protruding from the side of the wall. The stairs were partially obstructed by chunks of stone that had fallen upon them, and Charity carefully rolled the rocks and swept the gravel off of the stairs with her hands. "Look out below!" she said as the rocks and stones fell to the ground beneath them.

"Hey!" someone below them complained when a small rock hit them in the shoulder.

"Sorry," Charity said with a friendly wave.

At the top of the wall, several men aimed arrows down below. When the children scaled the wall, they gasped in awe at the size of the Roman army arrayed against the city. A Jewish archer eyed them with suspicion. "What are you doing up here?" he asked as he pulled back the string of his longbow to aim his arrow at a Roman soldier below.

Charity ignored him and gazed down at the battlefield below, looking for where she may have dropped her dagger. The siege towers got ominously closer, driving fear into the hearts of those who defended the wall. She looked to her left and saw that the Romans had slaves carrying buckets of dirt to the top of a huge mound they were erecting close to the wall. Charity figured that they were going to use this "earthwork" to lay a wooden bridge from it over the wall so that the soldiers could easily traverse the gap. About a hundred yards away from the battle, many soldiers and slaves were working together to completely surround the city with a second outer wall. They were trapping the Jews in the city, making escape impossible. She turned her attention to the muddy ground below, looking for the important dagger with the golden handle when an arrow sped past her head.

"Whoa!" Anna said, pulling Charity a little lower. "That was close."

"It's got to be down there somewhere," she said, standing again and pointing. "Help me look for it."

"Keep your head down," the Jewish soldier ordered, "or you're going to get yourself killed."

"We're all going to get ourselves killed anyway," the soldier beside him pessimistically remarked. "A Roman arrow in the head sounds like one of the better ways to go."

"Even if we see your dagger, how are we going to get it?" Daniel asked Charity.

Surprisingly, the Roman warriors began to pull their battering ram back away from the wall and retreated out of the range of the archers. The war-weary, famished Jews sounded a cheer that filled the smoky air.

Momentarily, a man dressed in a velvety maroon robe walked to the front of the line of Roman soldiers. He raised his hands heavenward, and everyone around him quieted. "Jerusalem!" he bellowed. "Have pity on the land of our forefathers! Why will you not surrender? Must it be completely desecrated? Can't you see that God has deserted Judea? Remember the words of Jeremiah. Surrender and live, or at least have a quick death! Refuse and you will perish miserably within those walls or be nailed to crosses outside of them!"

"Traitor!" many soldiers on the wall began to shout. "You have betrayed your people for the Roman pagans! You conspire to make the city of the Lord and His holy temple desolate!"

"You make it desolate yourselves!" he responded. "Titus sent me to urge you to relent your foolhardy defense of Jerusalem…"

"Who is that?" Charity asked the Jewish soldier beside him.

"That's Josephus, an infamous Jew who flattered Titus in order to save his own life. He's a traitor."

Charity turned and knelt beside Anna, Daniel, and little Johannine. Tears were in her eyes and her cheeks flushed with anxiety. Even if she could find her dagger and discover where James was being kept, and even if they could all touch the dagger at the same time and be ushered back home, what would happen to little Johannine? She looked at him, pitying him. "Johannine, you need to try to escape the city."

The Jewish solder overheard her admonition and interjected, "Even talking of such things will get you run through by the Zealots."

Everything was moving so fast. Charity knew that, apart from a miracle, they would not escape the coming onslaught. With one hand on Anna's shoulder and one hand on Daniel's back, she closed her eyes and began to pray fervently for help.

* * * * *

"Dig!" The hairy Zealot named Judah handed James a shovel and pointed at the end of the tunnel.

In obedience to John of Gischala's command, Judah had brought James into this tunnel from the back room of an old, dilapidated stone house that appeared to be abandoned. The black, narrow tunnel was dimly lit by a dozen oil lanterns that were fastened to the right side of the wall about every twenty yards. Wooden beams held the roof aloft, keeping it from collapsing on them. As the men and boys around James dug further, the wooden planks that held up the dirt ceiling bowed and looked as if the roof would collapse on them any moment. Dirt dripped down on them from the cracks between the planks.

"You'll get used to it," a boy beside James said.

James no longer felt like a fellow soldier who was needed by the radical band of guerilla warriors who occupied the temple. Now, he felt like a slave. "Why are we doing this?" James said as he stuck his shovel into the ground. His eyes were beginning to adjust to the dark environment.

The boy responded in a whisper, "Don't talk." The boy turned to cast a fearful glance at Judah, who sat on the ground about ten yards away. James saw a bloody red stripe across his bare back. James turned to face the Zealot who guarded them and saw a short leather whip attached to his belt.

"I am so thirsty," a young teen boy beside James complained. His body was void of the glistening sweat that James expected to see for one working so hard, evidence of his dehydration.

"No talking!" Judah responded, unlatching his whip and holding it with both hands. "Dig, and you'll get your water at the end of your shift."

* * * * *

When the huge battering ram struck the gate again, the stones beneath the children's feet buckled. As the archer beside them leaned over the wall to aim an arrow below, he lost his balance and toppled head first over the wall.

"The wall is crumbling!" another archer exclaimed worriedly.

The children fell to their knees as the wall swayed beneath them.

Several of the archers pushed the four children aside and fled down the stairs. The children followed a soldier that was bleeding from an arrow that had gone completely through the left side of his neck. Charity held him by the elbow as he hobbled down the stairs. Halfway down the stairs, the cemented stones beneath their feet cracked and gave way. The injured soldier in front of them fell head over heels off the ledge to the dirt road below. The road was filled with Jews either fleeing the impending breach of the gate, or rushing with weapons to defend their city from the soon-coming assault.

"Stop!" Charity told the children behind her as she balanced on the edge of the last stair that jutted out over a drop-off. She looked down and saw jagged rocks twenty feet below them. She suddenly slipped on some powdered rock and lost her balance when Daniel grabbed her skirt and pulled her back from the edge.

"Thanks, Daniel," she said, patting his sweaty arm. "You saved my life."

"Let's have a parade later," said Anna. "The wall's falling. We gotta jump…"

"No!" said Daniel. "You'll break your legs on those stones, or you'll land on somebody and hurt them."

"We cannot go back up," said Johannine, noticing how the upper part of the stairs had crumbled away.

"The gate is breaking!" a Levite shouted at the front of the line of Jews who stood in front of the weakening gate. "Get ready! For God and for Israel!" he shouted, his sword aloft.

"God be with us!" another screamed.

The Johnston children grew nauseated with the words. The hope the Israelites had apart from Christ was just as disheartening as the hopelessness of the families who cowered in their living rooms despairing.

The trembling of the wall seemed to still and everyone below them quieted, like the stillness before a tsunami. The squeaking of the wheels of the Romans' battering ram could be heard approaching the gate, picking up speed as the soldiers pushed with all their might.

When the battering ram struck the wall, it continued a dozen feet beyond the gate, splintering the thick wood and stretching the chains that covered the inside of the gate like a net. The Romans unleashed a roar of victory as loud as an approaching tornado, and fear snatched the breath out of the hungry Jews inside.

The wall trembled again, and the children clutched each other trying to keep the other from falling off of the stairs. They carefully maintained their balance on the teetering ledge.

"Do not retreat!" the Levite in the front shouted, trying to encourage the others. "There's no where left to flee, and there's no more food to sustain the siege. We must defeat them here!"

Many of the Jews began to shoot their arrows through the cracks in the wall, but the Romans were well concealed behind their shields and armor.

The Romans pulled their battering ram back and prepared to push it again toward the gate just as the first siege towers reached the wall. Romans began to step out on the precarious narrow ledge on the top of the wall, shooting their arrows down on the Jews. Many Jews began to scatter, rather than just stand there and be targets for the skilled Roman archers.

The three Johnstons and Johannine hugged the wall, trying to avoid being a target for the Roman archers above. Charity lifted her voice, "You're our shelter from the enemy, Jesus!"

"God, deliver us!" Anna began to pray.

Daniel and Johannine had their arms around each other, trying to balance on half of a stair that jutted out from the stone wall. "Jesus, help us," Daniel cried, his eyes lifted heavenward.

The battering ram struck the gate again, breaking it open. Shards of the chains that secured the gate shot out like shrapnel in all directions. Roman warriors flooded into the city like water through a broken dam, treading under foot the weakened Jews who tried to resist them. Jewish reinforcements were waiting in the alleys, and the Jews charged into the melee, swinging their swords and shooting their arrows with precision.

The side of the wall to which the four children clung weakened, and a whole chunk of the wall with the stairs slid down to the walkway below, taking the four children with it.

"Ah!" the children shrieked, falling to their backs against the stone.

The huge chunk of stone that swept them over the debris stayed intact until it slowed and struck a home. Then it shattered into a thousand jagged pieces of rock. The momentum of the four children flung them into the bushes on the side of the home.

Daniel was the first to rise to his feet, uninjured, and he began to help the others to stand as they cradled their scrapes and sprains. Johannine hit his head and was briefly knocked unconscious. When he came to, he was dizzy and nauseous. Charity was holding her knee with both hands, having sprained it badly.

"Be strong, Charity," Anna encouraged her as she helped her to her feet.

With the Romans clashing with armed Jews, the four children managed to duck away from the fighting and rush down a narrow alley between two houses.

Daniel, who was in the back of the line, looked over his shoulder and saw a line of Roman soldiers hot on their trail. "Hey!" Daniel hollered. "We're being followed! Faster!" he screamed. "They're catchin' up..."

"Follow me!" shouted Charity, running as fast as her sprained knee would allow. "I've got a plan!" She took a right down a narrow corridor between two rows of homes.

* * * * *

When the gate fell, a Jew in the corner of the courtyard screamed down a narrow road. "Collapse it now!"

A Jewish woman was waiting at the end of the road where it veered to the left. She turned, cupped her hands around her mouth to magnify her volume, and shouted, "Collapse it now!"

A man with his head outside of the window a hundred yards away heard her cry. He ran through his house and stuck his head out of a window on the other side of his home. "Collapse it now!" he screamed.

A Zealot, who sat on the outer wall of the temple, heard the command and sprinted to the entrance of the tunnel. He climbed into the tunnel and shouted, "Collapse it now!"

James heard the scream. "Collapse it? What?"

Judah stood to his feet. "Everybody out! Now!" Judah reached up and grabbed two oil lanterns that were on the wall beside him.

"What's happening?" asked James.

"Just leave!"

Judah threw the oil lanterns against the wooden posts that held up the ceilings, catching them on fire. He retreated out of the tunnel, and on the way he grabbed every oil lamp and broke it against the wooden post on which it hung.

The smoke of all the flames began to follow Judah and the diggers out of the tunnel. "Hurry!" Judah screamed between coughs. "Hurry!"

When the dozen men and boys reached the exit, soot covered their bodies, and black smoke stained their mouths and their noses.

"Here!" A Zealot was handing out swords as the diggers fled from the tunnel. "Go to the courtyard! To the courtyard!"

James was handed a dull double-edged broad sword that was as long as his leg. He grasped it in wonder as he followed the others out of the dilapidated shack and into the daylight. He squinted at the bright sun. He heard the chaotic shouting of fighting outside the temple and had the eerie thought that the sword would more likely cause his death than it would save his life. Oh, the thought of defending God's temple from the pagan Romans who sought to defile it!

* * * * *

The tunnel the Zealots had dug under the ground went all the way to the "earthwork" the Romans had erected outside the wall. When they burned the support beams, the tunnel collapsed, as did the huge mound of dirt and the wooden bridge the Romans had built to span the distance between the mound and the wall.

But the tunnel was also under the city wall, and when the mound collapsed into the ground, so did the wall. Now the whole Roman army rushed into the city of Jerusalem at once, determined to slay or enslave every inhabitant and lay the city waste.

* * * * *

"I can see the top of the temple!" The pain from Charity's sprained knee and the other children's bruises and scrapes eased as they zigzagged through the maze of homes and buildings.

Daniel was the slowest runner among the children, but fortunately the Roman soldiers who pursued them were weighed down with body armor, shields, and heavy broad swords or spears. He could hear the hurried breathing of the muscular Roman soldiers behind him as they drew nearer. He felt the wind of a passing sword just nick the back of his skull, cutting off a wisp of hair and creating a trickle of blood.

"Come here, you!" the Roman soldier hollered. Daniel's lungs began to wheeze, but he found the motivation to pick up his pace a bit.

"There's the temple!" Charity pointed as she ran. She began to holler James' name at the top of her voice. "James! James Vance Johnston! Where are you?"

They ran into the inner courtyard and Charity just barely ducked the swinging sword of a young Zealot. The young man saw that he almost struck a girl and he shouted, "Get out of the way girl!"

Anna, who was right behind Charity, entered the doorway more circumspectly, to avoid being struck, as did Johannine.

Within a few feet of the doorway to the temple court, Daniel felt a hand grab the upper part of his shirt. He was jerked off his feet and landed on his back, which knocked the breath out of him. "No," he frantically mouthed the words, but could not speak.

"I'm gonna disembowel you, Jewish scum!" The soldier raised his heavy broad sword and Daniel raised his hands as if to block it. The sword came down and Daniel closed his eyes.

A loud metallic clash sounded just above his face. He opened his eyes and saw that James had blocked the soldier's swing with his own sword!

The girls turned around from inside the temple courtyard to see their two brothers threatened by Roman warriors. "James! Daniel! Get in here!"

The Roman soldier raised his sword to beat down the young redhead who challenged him when an arrow, fired from close range, struck the soldier in the neck. The Roman soldier grabbed his neck and gurgled a noisy breath as he fell to his back. The optimism of the Roman soldiers wavered when they saw the enraged Zealots spill past the boys, clashing swords with the Roman soldiers.

James helped Daniel to his feet and pulled him inside the doorway that led to the courtyard just as they saw hundreds of fierce

Roman soldiers pour out from the small roads around the temple and rush toward them.

"Run!" said Charity and Anna simultaneously.

Charity led the way past the rows of Zealots who lunged into the battle. She fled up several wide stairs through a door in a wall in the center of the outer courtyard, which led to the inner court. All the Zealots had abandoned the temple for the conflict in the outer courtyard. They fled past two large pillars beside a tall, ornate door. They entered the inner sanctuary and paused to rest and to let their eyes adjust to the dim light. They walked through another doorway to enter a candlelit room with stairs that ascended to the small room that held the Ark of the Covenant. To their right was the golden candlestick, and to their left a table with bread and burning incense upon it. In front of the stairs was an altar for burning animal sacrifices.

"We can't go in here!" Johannine protested, yet followed anyway.

Daniel felt a strange stillness as they stood, breathing heavily, before a room he knew as the Holy of Holies. James' legs felt weak in this ancient holy room, and he used his sword as a crutch and leaned upon it.

"It's beautiful!" Anna exclaimed, her gaze fastening upon the blue, scarlet, and purple linen woven curtain that stood between them and the golden Ark.

Charity saw the awe in their countenances, and said, "The old covenant is ending, and the new covenant is beginning. Now God seeks to dwell in repentant hearts, not in golden boxes full of crumbled stones."

"Crumbled stones? Watch your mouth!" Anna protested what she supposed was Charity's disrespect of this holy place. "This is holy ground."

"Those stones are crumbled in more ways than one. Age hasn't broken the two tablets of stone that held the Ten Commandments, but do you think that God would let the Romans destroy this place if Jews hadn't trampled God's law?" Charity ascended the stairs and ran her fingers along the purple curtain. "This stopped being holy ground when this veil was rent from top to bottom, and an earthquake rocked this foundation the moment Jesus died. Now we enter the covenant through the blood of Jesus, not through the blood of animals and mercy seat on top of a golden box. This is a shadow, but we" – she took a deep breath and put her hands on the shoulders of Anna and James – "we have the reality this foretold. God's presence lives in us."

"It kind of makes me realize how much I've taken for granted in the new covenant," James commented.

Charity nodded. "Yeah."

The cries of the fighting neared outside of the room. "They're going to fight their way into here," said Johannine. "What are we going to do?"

"Die bravely," said James, holding his sword high and turning toward the entrance.

Two Roman soldiers, their arms and legs streaked with the blood of their enemies, rushed into the sanctuary. They halted as their eyes slowly adjusted to the darkness. James backed up, protecting his siblings with the sword. When they saw the children huddling together at the top of the stairs in front of the purple curtain, protected by a young boy with a dull sword, the soldiers approached.

"Oh God, help us," Charity prayed as she wrapped her arms around the children.

James, the only one armed, took a deep breath. "Well, if I'm gonna die, I might as well die bravely." He made his way down the stairs toward the soldiers. A Roman soldier swung his sword at James and he braced for the blow with both hands on the sword, but the Roman soldier was too strong. The sword was knocked out of his hands and spun across the air, clanging against the cedar wall and falling to the floor. The soldier then grabbed James by the scruff of his hair and flashed an evil grin. James thrust a fast kick at the soldier's stomach, but the solder pushed him away to avoid being kicked and James fell backward to the ground. The soldiers laughed at the helplessness of the five children. A tall man with a pale face entered the room, and the soldiers stopped laughing and stood at attention. This man looked like a king, dressed in a maroon robe. His wrists were covered with golden bracelets embedded with jewels.

The two soldiers bowed and smacked their forearms quickly against their chest. "Hail Titus!"

The Commander of the Roman legions stepped into the room, awed by the presence of the Ark of which he had only read. He glanced only briefly at the children. Two more soldiers entered right behind him. He slowly ascended the stairs as he unsheathed his sword.

"We're not Zealots, sir," said Anna.

"No, we're not even Jews," Charity added. "We were just—"

Without warning, the Commander swung the sword horizontally right above the children's heads.

They screamed and ducked, and the purple curtain behind them was cut by the Roman commander's sharp blade. Titus grinned when he saw the glitter of the yellow gold covered ark. "I'll tend it for you," Johannine said. He stepped forward. "I am a Jew, but I will clean it and protect it for you, with my life I will."

The soldiers laughed at the young Jew's audacity to speak so boldly in the presence of the son of Emperor Vespasian.

The Commander was curious. "Tell me, boy, what's in it?"

Johannine stood and, waving his arm like a salesman, said, "The Ten Commandments, Aaron's rod that budded, and a pot of the manna that fell from the sky in the wilderness after Israel's deliverance from Egypt."

The Commander grinned and moved closer to the curtain. The children moved aside so he could inspect his new prized possession. "Aaron's rod that budded? Tell me about the rod."

Johannine smiled, pleased that the Commander was finding him useful. "God confirmed the high priest Aaron's leadership over his competition by letting Aaron's walking stick bring forth live buds – just like you, sir." Johannine smiled at the Roman Commander. "God has given you the city of Jerusalem, you have the budding rod now." Titus appeared pleased with the comparison.

"What is manna?" Titus asked. The soldiers chuckled at the spontaneous history lesson, finding this brief repose from the violence of war refreshing.

"Well, sir, when Israel was in the wilderness after our exodus from Egypt—"

Suddenly, the curtain between the Holy of Holies and the sanctuary where they were standing was cut vertically, and three Zealots leapt through the slit in the curtain, screaming and swinging their swords at the Roman enemies.

One of them – John of Gischala – immediately killed the soldier who was nearest the children. Titus reached for Johannine, but Johannine backed up quickly against the wall to be with the children.

The three skilled Zealots engaged in intense mortal combat with the three Roman soldiers. They screamed as they swung their swords at each other with all their might. The Zealots vied for the once-in-a-lifetime opportunity to personally slay the Commander of the Roman legions, the son of the emperor!

A Zealot banged into the table and the golden candlestick fell and caught the cedar wooden panels in the wall on fire. The children were trapped between six clashing warriors in the inner court and the Holy of Holies as the flames slowly climbed the wall to their left.

As these elite soldiers tested their skills on each other, John of Gischala would not be undone. One of the Roman soldiers plunged his sword into the Zealot next to John, and taking advantage of the Roman soldier's inability to raise his sword to block John's blow, John brought his sword down quickly and thrust it through the soldier's neck. The Roman soldier fell hard sideways, knocking the soldier beside him over. John leapt and brought his sword straight down into the chest of the fallen Roman soldier with a mighty war cry. Some quick footwork and rapid thrusts of swords, and John of Gischala was the last Zealot standing, with one Roman soldier between him and the Commander of the Roman legions. The Commander was pinned in the corner of the room and unable to access the door.

"How do we get out?" Johannine squealed as fire crept across the ceiling.

"We're going to die in here!" Daniel fretted, clasping tightly to Anna's forearm.

Charity began to pray aloud. "Oh God, our enemy is too strong for us! Rise to defend your children…"

The Roman Commander darted for the door, but John of Gischala kicked the commander in the hip, causing him to fall against the doorway. He followed with a quick jab toward the last remaining Roman soldier, and delivered a deadly blow. The Roman fell to his knees and dropped his sword, but simultaneously reached for a dagger in a sheath on his right hip. Death took him before he could wield it. He fell to his face in a pool of his blood that reflected the flames engulfing the ceiling.

As John of Gischala and the commander faced each other, John's sweaty face beamed in the glory of war. He raised his sword and shouted, "For God and country!"

Little Johannine saw this as his only chance for survival. The Roman commander had smiled warmly at him, and he wanted to impress the Roman leader. Just as the Zealot began to swing his sword upon the Roman Commander, Johannine leapt onto the Zealot leader's back and wrapped his arms around his neck. James and Daniel would normally refuse to be outdone by another youngster in the throes of battle, but this was not make-believe and these were not play-swords. Besides, the children judged both sides of this conflict to be filled with evil men. They didn't consider either cause worth dying for. They were just looking for an opportunity to flee the room before it burned down with them in it. However, Johannine was their brother in the Lord, and they felt a strong connection to him. When John of Gischala raised his sword and prepared to scrape the blade across the head of Johannine, James jumped up and grabbed the Zealot's right arm. He wrapped both arms around the sweaty muscular forearm, and he pulled it down with all his might, bringing the tip of the sword to the ground.

"I'll kill you!" the Zealot fumed.

To be certain that the Commander wouldn't rise to his feet and flee the room, John of Gischala stepped toward Titus and delivered a swift kick in his face, knocking him senseless. Fearing for James' life, Charity and Anna each wrapped their bodies around one of the Zealot's legs.

"Get off me!"

James sunk his teeth into the man's wrist, causing him to growl a foul curse. Daniel grabbed the Zealot by the belt, and pulled him backwards. Unable to move his legs quickly enough, the Zealot fell to his back.

"Ah!" the Zealot leader screamed, his eyes wide with pain. John of Gischala reached back over his shoulder and screamed again. He rolled over and writhed as little Johannine continued to squeeze his neck. A dagger stuck out of his back, the dagger in the grasp of the dead Roman soldier. John of Gischala managed to reach back and pull out the knife, and in one last energetic burst, he swung it down at the child beside him, who was Daniel.

"Daniel!" Charity screamed.

James was horrified to see the knife protruding from Daniel's chest. Daniel fell onto his back in pain, but didn't have the breath to scream. John of Gischala, however, had breathed his last.

The Roman soldiers in the outer court soon defeated the last bastion of Zealots and discovered the conflict in the sanctuary that threatened the life of their Commander. Two soldiers stuck their heads into the sanctuary, but could not make out their commander from the smoke and flames that filled the upper part of the room.

Titus came to his senses and hobbled from the room. He ordered the two soldiers, "Save the boy! Save the boy choking the Zealot! He's important to me." The soldiers helped the Commander from the burning room and one of them reached in and grabbed Johannine by the scruff of his neck and dragged him out.

"What about the others?" a soldier turned to ask Titus. Their Commander had retreated to get care from his physician. A soldier behind him shouted, "Get out of there before it burns down."

"What about these other kids?"

"Let 'em burn!"

The two soldiers fled from the room, leaving the four Johnstons alone as the inner court and Holy of Holies became completely engulfed in flames. They began to cough from the dense smoke that filled every square inch of the room.

The three Johnstons surrounded Daniel on their knees, weeping for what seemed to be the last few moments of his life. Daniel's eyes dimmed as his breathing became more labored. It was then that Charity realized that the dagger in Daniel's chest was the same one she had dropped outside the city wall!

"The dagger!" Charity screamed and pointed at the dagger. "It's my dagger! The Roman soldier must have found it outside the city wall. Hurry! Touch it before Daniel dies!" They all reached for the dagger. Charity took one look over her shoulder at the Ark of the Covenant, its shiny gold reflecting the flames that engulfed the Holy of Holies.

Suddenly, the flames lost their heat, and began to spin around them in a refreshingly cool wind. The yellow storm of vibrant energy invigorated them instantly, and they found that their wounds were healed.

"Ah!" Daniel hollered, jumping to his feet and shouting praise to God. "Hallelujah! Praise God, I'm okay!"

The Johnstons huddled together, giving thanks for being spared.

The children began to absorb the gravity of what they had just witnessed. They clutched each other in fear and wonder. With tears in Charity's eyes, she repeated the words of Jesus Christ just before His crucifixion: "Ah, Jerusalem, Jerusalem. How oft would your Father have gathered you together, as a hen gathers her chicks under her wings, but ye would not. Now, your nation…" She paused to try to suppress the emotion that brought her to the edge of mournful weeping. "Now, your nation is left desolate."

In a moment, the fiery whirlwind slowed and they saw a purple sky was now above them.

"We're not going home yet," James said. "Look, there are no trees around, and it's a clear sky." When the whirlwind dissipated, they saw the beginning of a thrilling reddish orange sunset to the west. The stars were shining brightly above their heads, even though the sky still had some of the day's light left. Lines of smoke rose in the west made the sunset even more brilliant.

It was cold, and their quickened breaths were visible by the white mist that they expelled with every exhalation. To the east they saw a fleeing thunderstorm. They discovered that they were standing in the middle of a broad field of mud. To their horror, they discovered that dead or dying soldiers surrounded them, lying contorted on the icy mud. Some of them had hats of cloth on their head and others had shiny aluminum armor and helmets. Blood pooled on the ground under weapons haphazardly fallen all around in the mud, hardening into ice as the temperatures dropped. Arrows that had missed their target had stuck in the ground. They stood about fifty yards from a wide river, aghast at all of the death spread around them.

"What happened here?" Daniel wondered, hugging himself with his arms to still his shivering.

"Charity!" James pointed at his big sister's right hand. "The dagger. It's now a bow and arrow." She held them up in the air, and they were amazed at the finely polished bow and the sharpness of the arrow that had yellow-green feathers on the tip.

"Charge!" The cry came from what appeared to be every direction. The sudden roar of thousands of horse hooves slamming the icy mud slush chilled them to the bone. In both directions along the river, mounted horses charged each other with swords, spears, and bows. The four Johnstons found themselves in the middle of a bloody battlefield, with no place to hide.

Chapter 4

"**L**ook out!"

Charity's shout startled Daniel but he couldn't see what concerned her. She shoved him to the ground just in time. An arrow grazed his scalp just before he hit the dirt.

"Ow." Wetness dripped down his forehead. He rubbed at it, and his fingers came away covered with blood. More arrows struck the ground around them. Careful not to step into the path of a speeding arrow, Anna bent down to tend to him.

James was frantic. "We gotta get out of here!" The screaming voices, the blaring of war horns, and rumbling of the horse hooves neared. Charging cavalries crested the hills to the north and the south, descending quickly toward them, kicking up clumps of freezing mud in their wake.

"Run to the river!" Charity pointed at the swift-flowing, choppy waters to the west. "Come on!" She and James took off in a sprint.

"Let's go, Daniel!" Anna grabbed his hand and helped him to his feet, and then ran with him toward the river.

James and Charity hopped over a fallen log and waded ankle deep into the frigid water. They ducked behind some vegetation, hoping to make smaller targets for the soldiers.

"Oh! It's so cold." James shivered, finding the muddy brown water painfully cold against his legs.

Charity saw that Anna and Daniel were not going to make it before the cavalry clashed in battle all around them. She cupped her hands around her mouth to amplify her cry: "Run! Run!"

Anna saw the cavalry rushing toward them, with their heavy

curved swords and scimitars raised into the air. Men steadied their bows and took aim atop their muscular steeds.

"Faster Daniel!"

"I can't," he said, coughing. "I can't run any faster…"

A soldier with a red towel wrapped around his head raised his curved sword as he raced past the two short, pale-skinned enemies that impeded his progress. As his sword came down, Anna pushed Daniel to the ground away from her, letting the horse pass between them. Anna was on the side of the horse with the swinging sword, and that sword was about to cut off her head right when a spear pierced the man's chest, going all the way through him. He let go of the sword mid-swing, and it flipped through the air and stuck in the ground right beside Anna. The soldier fell off the horse on the opposite side of Anna, and landed on top of Daniel's legs.

Daniel wasn't injured by the man's fall, but he screamed nonetheless as the dark-skinned warrior groaned and bled on top of him.

The opposing cavalries collided all around them, and Anna hugged the ground to avoid the swinging of swords, and the arrows and spears flying over her head. The clash of steel and shrieks of the injured made Anna cover her ears with her hands, as if closing her mind to the chaos all around her would protect her from it. Anna dove to avoid the hooves of a huge, neighing horse. Heat from the swarm of beasts pressed in on her, and the stench of unwashed warriors assaulted her nostrils. She intently looked for any sign of Daniel through the haze of desperate warriors in mortal combat, but she could not see her little brother. She cried out for him, but he was pinned to the ground by a dying 220-pound horseman and could not hear her call.

"Anna! Daniel!" Charity and James screamed in horror when they lost sight of their brother and sister in the chaos. James began to move closer to shore, as if he intended to look for them in the maze of sweating horses, bleeding warriors, and clashing blades, but Charity grabbed him by the shirt and waded further into the freezing water to avoid attracting the eyes of those who may wish to kill them.

"I've got to go get them!" James opened his pocketknife in his right hand.

"No!" Panic whitened the skin on Charity's face. "Don't leave me alone."

"They're going to get killed, Charity. We can't just stay here and watch." James pulled himself out of Charity's grasp and sprinted into the battle behind the legs of a white horse as its rider traded sword swings with a rider of a black horse.

Charity was driven deeper into the river as the fighting of the cavalry forced some horses closer to the gravel bank of the river. "James!"

After passing a few battling warriors, James caught a glimpse Anna's flowing yellow-blonde hair through the legs of an armored horse. She sat on the ground beside the horse that had lost its rider, and was desperately searching for Daniel through the haze of flying mud sent into the air by stomping cavalry.

"Anna!" James called out to her, but she could not hear him. He screamed again: "Anna!"

She turned and locked gazes with James on the other side of the riderless horse. Tears filled her eyes. "I lost Daniel!"

"Get on the horse." James stood and grabbed the reins of the riderless horse. "We gotta get outta here!"

Anna leapt on the horse and took the reins from James. She reached down with her right hand and helped James up on the horse's back.

James grabbed Anna around the waist. "Go!" Anna banked the horse sharply toward the river, trying to bypass the combating warriors.

Anna could see Charity's face above a branch of a bush on the river's edge, and the look of fear on Charity's face made Anna's hair stand on end. Charity screamed, "Look out, Anna!"

A dark-skinned warrior lifted a spear to throw at Anna, and it struck her horse in the neck. The horse rose up on its back legs and bucked off its riders. Anna tried to sit up, but her leg was trapped underneath the fallen horse. Between James and Anna was a dark-skinned warrior, drunk with rage. Anna saw that his scimitar was poised to deliver the fatal strike against her.

"No!" James ran and used the horse's chest as a launching pad to dive at the warrior. He plunged his pocketknife into the man's spine.

The warrior staggered, and then recovered. He tried to reach for the knife sticking out of his back but could not. The warrior turned to James, and Anna saw that her brother was now weaponless and face-to-face with an armed warrior. She pushed the horse's hind legs off of her with all her might.

"You miserable infidel!" The warrior's black eyes blazed with hatred when he saw the orange-headed boy. He coughed blood onto his black beard, raised his curved sword high above his head, and screamed a blood-curdling shriek, "Allah Akbar!"

Surrounded by swinging swords and stomping horses, James had nowhere to run.

Anna freed herself from the fallen horse and jumped up on the back of the dark-skinned warrior just as he prepared to wield his sword against her brother. She tried to wrap her arms around his neck. "I'll 'allah' your 'akbar'." He dropped his scimitar and lost his balance momentarily. Then he reached up and grabbed a fistful of Anna's hair, causing her to scream. He bent forward to try to throw the feisty enemy off of his back.

James leaped and struck the warrior in the chin with his knee shouting a mighty "Heeeahh!" Anna let go of the warrior's neck as he crumpled to the ground with a broken jaw. She gazed over James' shoulder to see another warrior approach James from behind. This warrior had a braided black beard and growled like a mad beast. He wore a bright orange hat that revealed his high rank in the cavalry. He cocked his spear and prepared to thrust through the albino midget-warrior with all his might.

Charity saw that James was about to be killed. She only had one arrow in her hand and James was on the other side of the warrior, so she took careful aim. Charity sent her arrow straight into the back of the warrior. The point of the arrow went right through his chest, causing him to drop his spear and fall toward James.

"Aahh!" James shouted when the warrior in the bright orange hat fell on top of him. James fell to his back and held the dying warrior up with his hands to keep the point of the arrow from sinking into his own abdomen.

The dark-skinned warriors all around them began to push back the pale-skinned warriors. Charity cupped her hands around her mouth and shouted, "Get out of there!"

Anna bent to help push the dead Muslim warrior off of James. James pulled his knife out of the other soldier's back, and then he and Anna ran toward Charity as fast as their legs would go. They jumped a fallen log just as Charity slipped on the slimy rocks underneath her feet into the frigid, rushing river water.

"Charity! Where'd she go?"

Charity could swim well, even one-handed, as she held fast to the bow with her other hand. But the current was strong and it pulled her down into the wintry river. Before she could swim back up to the surface, her shirt got caught on the branch of a submerged tree and kept her trapped under the icy waters. She could not swim up to get a breath of air! She pulled against the tree with all of her might, but it held fast.

Fear zipped up Anna's spine. Where was her sister? "Charity! Charity!" She scanned the water's surface, and saw a hand waving just a few inches above the shallow waves. "There she is!" The hand went down into the water and then back above the water again, waving frantically. "She's underwater! She's stuck. She's gonna drown!"

James and Anna swam to her as fast as they could. Anna took a deep breath and dropped into the muddy water. She quickly discovered that the branch of the submerged tree had trapped her big sister beneath the water's surface.

Anna came back up for a deep breath of air. "She's snagged on a branch!"

She and James took a deep breath and plunged into the cold brown water. She began to pull and tug at the branch, but it was a freshly sunken tree and the branch was too green and rubbery and would not break easily. James opened his pocketknife and began cutting at her shirt to try to free her.

Anna came to the surface, took another deep breath of air, then went back down and put her lips to Charity's lips. She breathed out as Charity breathed in. Her sister's lungs filled with refreshing, life-giving air. When Anna resurfaced for another breath of air, she saw Muslim warriors aiming their arrows at them from atop their horses. Quickly, she drew in another deep breath and barely missed being hit by a speeding, razor-sharp arrow.

James finally cut a hole in Charity's shirt, and they all swam to the surface, only to find arrows whizzing all around their heads and splashing into the water.

Charity gasped and took a deep breath of air. Anna tried to calm her exhausted sister as she held her up to the surface.

"Take a deep breath," James screamed, "and try to swim across the river underwater! Come on!"

They each took a deep breath of air and plunged into the frigid water to swim away as fast as they could. But an arrow sliced through Anna's ear, causing her to gasp and inhale a mouthful of water. She rushed to the surface, gagging and coughing.

Fortunately, the Muslim warriors raced off into the direction of the action, and the risk of being shot from shore subsided.

"Are you okay?" James swam toward Anna and helped keep her

afloat as they assessed her injury.

"It's just a nick," Charity said as she examined the laceration in Anna's ear lobe. "That's what you get for giving me mouth-to-mouth."

"Well, I'm sorry. You know, I left my oxygen tank in Zanesville." They all laughed at Anna's humor, but the speed of the river current soon made them realize they were still very much in danger.

After several minutes of hard swimming, they finally made it across the river, the river's strong current made it difficult to pull themselves up the steep, muddy bank. A young man was riding his horse fast along a trail beside the river when he saw the three strangers struggling to make it to shore. He stopped his horse, lowered his black cape for them to grasp, and helped them up to dry land one by one.

Charity, Anna, and James shivered in the freezing cold as they stood on the bank, their eyes fixed to the scene across the wide river. Their wet clothes grew stiff on their shivering bodies as they watched the dark-skinned warriors overwhelm the smaller force of pale-skinned warriors. Where was their little brother?

"Oh, Daniel! Daniel!" Anna's mournful cry put into words what they all felt. Tears flooded their eyes and froze fast to their cheeks. They watched in the darkening evening as the Muslim warriors left off pursuit of the fleeing force of pale-skinned warriors and returned to plunder the dead and injured by torchlight.

"Let's pray for his safety." James fell to his knees and began to pray fervently for Daniel to be kept safe.

Anna wiped her tears and took a deep breath. "Yes. God saved me in the Philistine camp. God is able to save him too." She and Charity dropped to their knees beside him.

The young man in the black cape had mounted his horse and was preparing to continue on his mission, but he was saddened as he watched the grief of the three young shivering children on the side of the bank. He knew that they barely escaped with their lives, and from their mourning he discerned that they had lost a loved one in the battle. Their quickness to go to God in prayer moved him.

The young man sighed heavily as he watched the Islamic invaders across the river push back his fellow warriors. "I suppose the intelligence I've gained can wait until morning." He jumped off his horse and began to gather sticks on the ground. "You three are freezing. Let me get a fire going."

* * * * *

Soon after the man had fallen off his horse onto Daniel's legs, the ankle of a trotting horse bumped into Daniel's forehead and he was knocked unconscious by the collision. When he awoke, his head ached terribly. The blood on his hands reminded him of how the arrow had just skimmed his scalp. The soldier that had fallen on top of his legs was still there, stiff and lifeless.

He pushed the dead soldier off of him and one of the plunderers, who emptied the pockets and pouches of the dead and dying, came up to him and pushed him back to the ground.

"What are you doing?" Daniel inquired as the dark-skinned man rolled him over and began to tie his wrists behind his back. "What do you want? Where am I? Where are my sisters and my brother?" All of his questions went unanswered.

The dark-skinned man lifted Daniel to a standing position, and began to pull him along the river toward their camp. After several minutes walking through a maze of dead horses and men, Daniel saw tens of thousands of white tents in the distance. "Where are you taking me?"

"I am taking you to your new school."

"School? I already go to school. I'm home-schooled."

"Are you educated in the Koran?"

"In what's wrong with it. We study the Bible, sir. Do you know about Jesus?"

Daniel's captor stopped, turned, and grinned at the yellow-headed boy with the streak of blood from a head laceration and a black eye. Then he delivered a swift slap against the unbruised side of Daniel's face. The palm smacked his ear and made him go deaf for a moment. Daniel winced and braced for another. He looked up at his assailant and saw a crooked smile on his face.

"I'm impressed with your courage and boldness, but you're going to bring trouble to yourself if you don't accept your new position in life." The man suddenly tugged at Daniel's bound wrists, almost causing him to stumble. "Welcome to the rule of the merciful and compassionate Allah, blessed be his name." His captor continued to pull him by the wrist-cuffs toward their camp. "You're going to get a dawn-to-dusk crash course in your new religion under new tutors. If you're fortunate, you'll get sold to a Muslim owner next week."

* * * * *

"He's dead. You'll never see him again." By the warmth of the small fire, the young man in the black cape tried to convince the three children that their brother could not have survived the clash of warring cavalry.

Charity, Anna, and James huddled closely to the fire to warm their freezing, wet bodies. But their faith was not chilled by the circumstances. They refused to believe that Daniel had been killed across the river. "Well, if Daniel were alive," said Charity, "where would he be?"

The young man shook his head, as if he feared that an honest answer would revive the pitiful grief of the three strangers. After a heavy sigh, he said, "They have a caravan of slave-traders that comes through the enemy's camp to pick up captured slaves and take them throughout the Muslim empire to sell. Don't hold out hope for your brother. Even if he did survive—"

"Captured slaves?" Anna squealed. "He's gonna be a slave?"

"And that's the best you can hope for."

James took off his shirt and laid it on the rocks around the fire. "Where do they keep the slaves until they are sold?"

"They are forced to convert to Islam and memorize the Koran. They'll be in the enemy's camp, well guarded."

Those words gave Anna a nauseating déjà vu sensation, as she recalled being tied up in the Philistine camp in the valley of Elah. Her thoughts went to the thousands of Jews that were enslaved when Jerusalem fell to the Romans, and a sick feeling aroused from deep within her. Anna hugged her shoulders, shivering now more from anxiety than from the cold. "What is your name?"

"Sir John."

Charity, Anna, and James looked at each other wide-eyed. Johnny's gun had gotten them into this trip through time, and Jonathan, the son of King Saul, returned the slingshot to them that ushered them out of the valley of Elah. Johannine, which was a Jewish rendition of the name John, had helped save their lives in the temple. Maybe Sir John was the key to getting them home.

"What were they fighting over?" Charity asked as she motioned across the river.

"The Muslims want to conquer us and make us Muslim, and we want to stay free and stay Christian. We Franks are foot-soldiers, but we managed to get enough horses to mount a resistance. As you saw, we didn't do very well. The real battle's just about to get started. That Muslim army," Sir John said, pointing downstream, "has expanded into the largest empire since Christ. The Byzantine and Persian empires fell to them easily."

"What year is it?"

Sir John looked at Charity as if she were crazy. "The year of our Lord, 732. October. Why?"

Charity glanced at her siblings with her jaw agape.

James leaned forward with his elbows on his knees and his eyes firmly fixed on Sir John's face. "How do you intend to stop the Muslims?"

The young man prodded the fire with a stick. "The Consul of Gaul, Charles Martel, has united enough Frankish and Burgundian forces to put up a good fight against the Umayyad invaders." He pointed northwest with the glowing point of his stick and rested his other hand on his sheathed sword. He then pointed downstream. "The Umayyads have plundered, murdered, enslaved, and raped nation after Christian nation. Their cavalry has been invincible."

"Has anyone tried to make peace with them?" Anna edged closer to the fire and stretched her palms toward its warm radiance.

Sir John half chuckled and half balked at the question. "You're kidding, right? You can't make peace with Islam. Their religion demands submission and it expands by military conquest. From the very beginning, Mohammed's following grew through violence. Muslims hate Christians because Christianity teaches that Jesus is God's Son and the Koran says that God does not have a Son. The Umayyads will not rest until they have killed or converted every

Christian. They have, up to this point, been unstoppable."

"What makes you think you can stop them?" Anna asked. "How can foot-soldiers withstand experienced warriors on armored horses?"

"With God's help. That's how. If we don't stop them here, our children and grandchildren will be slaughtered or made slaves for generations, from Tours all the way to the great ocean!"

The Johnston children were filled with wonder. Why were they here? What was happening? What was God's purpose in all this?

"What do you mean, the great ocean?" James asked.

Charity answered the question. "The Atlantic Ocean. We are on the eve of the Battle of Tours. Christopher Columbus, George Washington, and Patrick Henry were Christians, not Muslims, due in part to the victory at the battle of Tours."

Sir John was confused. "Victory at the Battle of Tours? You speak as if tomorrow's battle has already happened." He looked at her for a moment as if she were insane.

"Where's this Christian army now?"

Sir John pointed the direction from which the river flowed. "Follow me to camp tomorrow morning, and I'll show you."

James shook his head and looked at Charity and Anna. "I can't go with you. I've got to find Daniel."

"What?!" Charity and Anna exclaimed simultaneously.

"You haven't forgotten about Daniel, have you? He could be sold by tomorrow morning as far as we know. He's—"

"Your friend's dead. Accept it." Sir John sounded cold, and James turned away from him toward the river as if he found his counsel offensive. "Accept the inevitable and abandon this insane mission."

"If he is alive," James responded without looking at him, "I will find him and help free him."

"If you try to find him, you will be killed or captured yourself, and forced to convert to Islam."

"No way," James said as he shook his head vigorously. "They will never make me turn my back on Jesus."

"They will torture you!"

"And that's why I must find Daniel, to make sure he keeps his faith. I will find him if I have to sell myself into slavery, like the

Moravians did."

That comment made Sir John laugh out loud. "Very funny."

James' gaze darted to the young man in the black cape, his brow furrowed and his tone unbending. "I wasn't kidding."

"And how are we going to get home then?" Anna could not conceal the fear in her voice.

"How are we going to get home without Daniel? Without Daniel we—" Charity froze in mid-sentence, her face growing even paler by the light of the fire.

Anna's heart skipped a beat at the sight of Charity's frightful gasp. "What is it, Charity?"

"A cold, hard fact just stung me. I have made a terrible mistake."

"What?"

"The arrow. I shot that Muslim wearing the orange hat with my only arrow to save Anna. You're right, James. You have to go back to the Muslim camp. But not just to find Daniel. You've got to find Daniel *and* that arrow that's stuck in the chest of that dead warrior, or none of us will *ever* make it home."

"What?" Sir John stood to his feet, disturbed with the insistence of these children to march into the camp of the Umayyad warriors. "They burn their dead. Why this sentimental obsession with an arrow? It's futile! I'll give you some more arrows."

"The arrow's special," Charity insisted. She rolled her eyes toward the black sky. "You wouldn't understand."

Sir John pointed his stick with the orange-glowing tip at Charity, and raised his voice. "Give it up! You'll *never* find that arrow. You'll *never* find your brother."

Anna's free-flowing tears transformed into a heart-wrenching sob. "Oh no! We'll never make it home." Anna's emotion burst the dam of Charity's grief. Now both girls were sobbing.

James put his hands on the shoulders of his sisters and tried to make eye contact with them. His smile was quite out of place. "It's a small thing for God, sisters. Don't mourn as if we've lost Daniel already. The great cloud of witnesses above," he said, pointing heavenward, "are buying tickets to watch this. God will give us the victory if we believe."

As Sir John listened to James' encouraging words, his whole countenance changed. He began to clap. His applause was robust and prolonged. "Amen!" he shouted as he put his head back and laughed. "Amen! I have never seen such bravery among warriors so small. I am so glad to have met you. How can tyrants survive in such an atmosphere of faith? I feel like I could take on the whole Umayyad army myself now!"

* * * * *

"You will stay in here!" One of the spiritual leaders of the invading army, the chief Muslim imam, thrust Daniel to the floor in the holding cell. "No food. No water. Not until you submit to Allah and begin to learn the Koran."

"I'll be glad to learn it, but I'm always going to be a Christian." The bars were slammed shut on the back of the small barred compartment, which was affixed to a horse drawn carriage. Inside this small jail cell, which was covered with bars on all sides, were six other stubborn Christian boys and girls who refused to submit to their Muslim captors. They huddled and whimpered in the corner. The cruel imam locked the door and disappeared down the dark trail toward his tent in the dusk of the cold evening.

Daniel was immediately overwhelmed by the putrid smell of human waste and filth. He looked up toward heaven, the bright stars of the seventh century obscured only by the white mist of his breath in the wintry evening of the northern European October.

He turned and faced the six other children, and gave them a wide smile. "Hi. I'm Daniel." He introduced himself to each of them and sat down in their midst. He patted a five-year-old girl on her shoulder. "You don't need to be scared."

"Our parents are dead," she mourned through chattering teeth. "Now, they're going to force us to be Muslims."

Daniel pointed to the star-studded sky. "Nah, they aren't dead. They're in heaven right now watching you. They're proud of you. If you will be faithful to Jesus, you'll be with them some day." Daniel saw a faint smile shine upon her thin lips, and he placed an arm over her shoulders. "Don't be afraid. God is with us."

* * * * *

James left his sisters, swam back across the river, and snuck along the muddy bank of the river for three miles into the wee hours of the morning. He was cold, exhausted, and covered with mud when he caught sight of some warriors gathered around a small campfire on the bank. He crawled close to them on his hands and knees in ankle-deep water so he could overhear the conversation of the elaborately dressed generals and captains. He drew so close to them he could smell the scent of the strong coffee they sipped around the fire, but he could only barely overhear them from the chattering of his teeth.

"We will not retreat!" The man who spoke around the dim camp-fire wore a bright orange coat decked with jewelry. He had a broad sword sheathed at his waist and elaborate golden daggers sheathed and strapped to both of his thighs. "I shall not bear the shame of it. It is not an option. The infidel army is somewhere near here - I know it!" He pointed toward the unconquered terroritory to the west, and then took another sip from his mug.

"General Abdul, we are in their country and have moved far quicker than our supply train could safely travel." A thick-shoul-dered black-eyed warrior with a red turban dared to propose a reality check of the general's ambition. "We are not prepared for this bitter winter that is rapidly coming upon us. They will outlast us."

"No, they will not." General Abdul was insistent.

A fat chief with a ring through his nose tossed a few logs of wood in the fire. "Our raids will sustain us. When the leaders of this Christian army see their children being led away in chains, they will come out from the shadows of the mountains and face us. They have no standing army. These are farmers and sheep-herders, not profes-sional warriors. We are seasoned with the blood of many enemies in many conquests."

"We have too great a burden of treasure and our supply lines are being raided too frequently. We don't even know the location or the strength of our lurking enemy. We must return to fight later, when we have more knowledge of our opposition and when the weather is more becoming."

"Shall I be scared of phantoms and snowflakes?" The sharp-jawed General Abdul stood to his feet as he began to upbraid the captain with the red turban. "You disgust me! I shall need to kill a few slaves in order to clean the bad taste out of my mouth which you have given me with your fears and tears. No more of this cow-ardice! The armies of Allah will *not* retreat! We *will* sack Tours, we *will* burn their churches, raid their homes, loot their storehouses, and enslave their wives and children." He made a tight fist with his right hand. "We *will* continue our advancement west, sending our trea-sure and our slaves back east through better fortified caravans. If it snows, we will burn their homes for warmth. Allah be praised." He unsheathed his scimitar and extended it toward the fire, causing his men to flinch as if they feared he would strike at them in his wrath. "Weep not because you miss your wives and your velvet couches – not in my army." He shook his sword in their faces. "We hunger for the pleasures of Allah's paradise, not the swine of this world. We will make Europe Muslim. We will not fail!"

That was all the convincing they required. They joined in a unified roar of enthusiastic agreement with their famed general's ambitious plans.

* * * * *

"We will have the element of surprise and the choice of ground. That will give us an advantage." Charles Martel, the Consul of Austrasia counseled with his chiefs and leaders of the militia forces before daybreak. "Avoiding the roads, we will come up to his neck when he least expects it. We must pick our ground carefully. They have amassed somewhere along this river." He pointed at the Vienne River on a chart with a long, thin stick. "My scouts are at this minute returning and hopefully bearing news of the location of his primary force."

"I can barely restrain my men in these hills and woods." A local militia leader raised his voice in frustration to protest the Consul's reluctance to attack. "Some of our homes have been burned, and some of our wives and children kidnapped. We should move more quickly by way of the old Roman roads. We should quit hiding in these hills and engage them now." He pounded a fist into his palm.

Martel crossed his thick, muscular arms across his broad chest. "The impatient can join the raiding parties and harass supply trains."

"No, we want to destroy this Umayyad army once and for all, Consul! We weary of small victories in small skirmishes. The fate of the Christian religion depends on destroying this army, not merely sending them to flee so they can recover and return later. Let us pull our forces into the plains, and draw out the invaders."

"That won't work. They far outnumber us and they have

cavalry while we do not. We will not win unless we are strategic in our defenses."

Sir John, the young scout, stepped into the Consul's tent with Charity and Anna right behind him.

"Sir John!" the Consul said when he caught sight of him. "Better late than never."

"A thousand pardons, Consul. Citizens at peril of their life required my aid." The young man motioned to Charity and Anna, who stood at the door of the tent behind him. "But I am here to report that eighty thousand Umayyad warriors have gathered on the other side of this very mountain, and are totally unaware of our presence."

His jaw dropped open and the other captains and leaders gasped. "Eighty thousand? That close?"

The Consul moved closer to him and pointed his thin stick at the young man. "Are you sure of this?"

"Their warriors rest in their tents while their chiefs bathe on the sandbar where the Clain and Vienne Rivers join. One of our raiding parties interrogated a Muslim scout that had been captured east of here, Consul. I heard him myself. They conspire to invade and raid as they cling to their spoils and treasure, but they have no knowledge of our presence or the number of our forces."

A mighty cheer erupted in the tent, silenced by the raised hand of their somber Consul. "Not so fast. Eighty thousand experienced warriors is almost three times our number of amateurs." The general shook his head, regret etched on his features. "We cannot take on that many and win. Especially with their cavalry."

"And their cavalry is very strong."

"Yes, I learned of last night's embarrassing cavalry skirmish." The Consul began to pace around the room. "That's what impatience gets us, men. An embarrassing defeat and an encouraged enemy."

Sir John pointed to the location on the map where their enemies were amassing. "That's where they camp."

"Maybe we can divide them and then engage half of their army at a time," an elderly captain proposed.

The Consul bit his lip and turned to face the gray-headed captain. "No. We couldn't beat half their force. I don't see how we can win this under these circumstances."

"I have an idea," came the soft, unexpected effeminate voice in the corner of the room. It was Charity. She stepped forward and every eye fastened on her. The room full of captains and leaders balked at the girl who dared to counsel them.

"And you are?"

"Charity, and this is my sister Anna. May I make a proposal?"

A burly guard at the door of the tent reproved her, "Why do you so boldly presume to speak in this room? Where are you from?"

"We are from the United States, and were caught in the battle last night, and–"

"You belong with the children, not in the tent of men of war! Get out of here!"

Charity objected to the spurning of the irritable guard beside her. "God has chosen the foolish things of this world to confound the wise, and the weak things to confound the mighty. Josiah was eight, sir, when he was made king of Israel. Paul told Timothy to let no man despise his youth."

The Consul grew curious. "Tell me of your country, this United States. I have never heard of it."

"We used to be a nation that served the Lord Jesus Christ and abided by His law."

"Used to be?"

"Yes sir. We have departed from God."

The Consul glanced at the generals and captains that filled his tent. "A nation that forgets God will be turned into hell, ma'am."

Anna nodded in agreement as she stepped up beside her sister. "And that is what's happening to us. We have been attacked by the same kind of jihadists that afflict you. With God's blessing, you will overcome in spite of the odds, but without God's blessing, you may lose even if the odds are in your favor."

"So your idea to counter the enemy is to pray for God's blessing?" Martel shook his head as some of his chiefs grinned at their Consul's caricature. "That's it?"

"What my sister's trying to say, Consul," Charity spoke up, "is that God's blessing is more critical to victory than the numbers you lack. Six of the seven churches mentioned in chapters two and three of Revelation were destroyed by the Muslim armies. Not because they were unarmed or unprepared for war, but because the salt lost its savor. Because they left their first love and became lukewarm in their faith. God will give us freedom if we're worthy of it."

The Consul took a deep breath as an uneasy moment passed. Anna and Charity felt the presence of the Lord in that tent, and they knew that God had spoken through them.

"Truly," said the Consul, "you both speak the truth." He looked around at his chiefs, generals, and captains. "Echo these words to your men. Let not their desire for vengeance on the Muslims distract them from their duty to God, for ultimately the battle and the victory belong to the Lord, and He rewards those who diligently seek Him. Have all your men confess their sins to God and implore Him for the victory."

"Yes Consul."

"Consul, I have a plan you may wish to consider." Charity stepped to the drawing board and pointed at a place by the river. "Yesterday, I witnessed the invaders leave off pursuit of a defeated group of fleeing militia in order to plunder pockets of the dead and injured. From what Sir John has told me, this army has plundered and looted hundreds of towns and is fat with treasure. You have harassed their caravans, which means they are reluctant to send their riches back without their forces to guard them. We can use that lust to our advantage."

"How?"

* * * * *

At the break of dawn, Martel led his troops quietly over the mountain, where they huddled together in the shadows of the trees, rocks, and hills as the far superior Umayyad forces awoke to orders to march to the city of Tours. Martel's forces watched as the horde of Muslim warriors marched northward in the plains below.

A scout rushed to the Consul and reported: "The Umayyad have left very few forces to guard their slaves and their treasure. They do not know we are here."

"Very well. Tell Benham, Trewhella, and Newman's companies to follow me down the slopes in ten minutes from right now. Have the rest follow close, as one. But tell them that under no circumstances are they to drop into the plains. We must draw the enemy cavalry up into these hills."

"Yes sir!" The scout turned his horse and galloped away on a mountain trail.

"You!" The Consul pointed at another messenger on horseback. "Tell Sir John to commence his raid of the enemy's camp. And tell the two young women with him that I wish them well in their search for their lost brother."

* * * * *

"Charge!" Sir John's shout echoed off the gently sloping hillside.

The thousand militia that flanked him on both sides left the cover of the bushes and trees and rushed toward the sparsely defended Umayyads' camp. Charity and Anna were right behind Sir John, praying silently for James and Daniel, who they prayed were somewhere in the vast fields of tents and servants sprawled out on the plains beyond them as far as they could see.

* * * * *

"Now sir? Now?"

Consul Charles Martel's heart throbbed with anticipation. If all his life came down to one moment, this would be his moment, his greatest exploit. He remembered what was at stake, and his thoughts went to his wife and children, to his unborn grandchildren and great grandchildren. He tried to imagine them as slaves in a Muslim world. Our faith puts God on the spot, and affords Him an opportunity to show Himself strong on behalf of those whose hearts are pure.

"Now, Consul? It's been ten minutes."

The Consul swallowed hard. The largest part of the Umayyad army was right below them. "Now!"

* * * * *

A messenger galloped quickly toward General Abdul, shouting as he neared. "General Abdul! General Abdul! An army is coming down from the mountain." He pointed up the mountain and the general squinted to see through the morning fog.

"How many?"

"I cannot ascertain. They are at least five hundred footmen wide, with steeper banks on each side of them. They are stopping at the treeline and their numbers are concealed by the forest. They are not attacking. They have the high ground."

"Any cavalry?"

"No sir."

The general grinned sadistically, showing his coffee-bean stained teeth. He patted his white stallion, evoking a proud neigh from the mighty beast. "On this day we shall see Allah's greatest victory." He raised his scimitar high into the air, and his commanding voice thundered throughout the valley. "Send the cavalry up the mountain! Full frontal assault!"

"Yes General!"

* * * * *

Charity and Anna rushed behind Sir John's forces, searching tents for James and Daniel as they went. Charity had her bow, and Sir John had given her a quiver full of arrows, which was slung over her shoulder. Anna was unarmed at the onset, but she soon picked up the dropped scimitar of a fleeing Arab. The Arabs that remained at camp seemed more concerned about piling whatever wealth they could on their horses and heading south than in fighting the small band of pale-skinned marauders. It wasn't long until a heated battle broke out.

Charity and Anna stopped a teenage servant girl who was running on foot away from the conflict. Charity poked her bow in her chest. "Where are the other slaves?"

The girl backed away from them and Charity pursued her until the girl fell on the ground, whimpering. "Where would they keep the slaves they captured yesterday?"

She pointed to the east. "At the edge of the camp, farthest away from the battleline."

Charity and Anna began to sprint past the tents, trying to keep their distance from many Arabs who also sprinted in the same direction. Suddenly, an orange-headed boy burst out of a tent and ran right into Charity. They crashed into one another and fell to the ground with a grunt.

"Ow! James! You're always crashin' into people!" Charity brushed herself off and tried to get back onto her feet.

"Sorry. I'm glad to see you too." He stooped to help her up.

"James!" Anna smiled and gave him a hug. "Have you found Daniel?"

James looked over Charity's shoulder and suddenly pushed her to the ground. A long-bearded Arab warrior was about to plunge his sword into Charity's back.

"James!" Charity protested James' shove until she felt a pain in her hip; then she understood why James had pushed her. The Muslim warrior managed to lacerate Charity's hip just as she was pushed aside, and then sunk the point of his sword into James' thigh.

"Ah!" Charity screamed, more from fear than from pain.

James unsheathed the sword he had found in an abandoned tent and thrust the young Arab through with it. He then put his foot up on the warrior's chest and kicked him away.

"Are you all right, James?" Anna waved her sword against anyone who drew too near to them.

James mouth gaped open wide as he hopped around for a moment before crumpling to the ground and exhaling a howl of misery. Anna wasn't sure if he was mortally injured or was just playing the "Drama King" as he occasionally did, making a big deal of nothing. She bent down to examine the nick in James' thigh. When James saw that it was only a small cut, he took a deep breath and gritted his teeth. "It doesn't hurt bad. I'll be all right."

"I'm bleeding worse than you are." Charity grasped her hip as she carefully stood to her feet.

James slowly stood up and took up the fallen warrior's sword so that he now held one in each hand. "Can you run Charity?"

"I think so." She began to move her leg around to test it. Just inside the tent beside them, she noticed an abandoned hatchet lying on the ground. She picked it up and put it through her belt. "Where's Daniel?"

"Follow me." James took off eastward with a limp in his gait, but his speed was not in the least bit diminished.

* * * * *

The armored cavalry galloped up the hill toward Martel's forces as fast as they could, the mighty roar of enraged shouting echoing through the hills and valleys. The militia lined up shoulder-to-shoulder in a phalanx formation. The shield in the left hand of each soldier protected the right side of the body of the soldier to his left. The rows of infantry behind the front line pressed against the row in front of them, to help stop the charging cavalry from just running right through them. The soldiers in the second and third rows wielded long spears, which they thrust at the enemy over the backs and shields of the men in front of them. Reinforcements behind them quickly filled any gaps in the wall.

The cavalry galloped uphill against the rocky, steep terrain, and was halted against the immovable wall of determined, Christian warriors. The cavalry could not pierce their defenses. These militiamen had the terrain in their favor, and even better they had Jesus Christ on their side. Worst case scenario, they were going to heaven. When the cavalry began to suffer casualties from the spears wielded by the men in the second row of the phalanx, they turned their horses and retreated back down the mountain. It took all of the discipline the militia could muster to keep from rushing down upon the enemy when they fled.

At the bottom of the mountain, the cavalry reformed their lines, and the call to charge sounded again. The cycle repeated with the wall of courageous Christian warriors repelling the charging cavalry over and over again. With every attempt of the cavalry to flank their position, reinforcements would drop down out of the woods to repel the charge.

"Hold your position!" Charles Martel ordered from the center of the tightly packed defensive formation.

"They're retreating, Consul! We should attack."

"No! Hold your ground. There are still too many. Keep the phalanx intact. Let us pray that the attack on their camp will divide their forces."

* * * * *

The chief of the Muslim cavalry panted from leading his men

up and down the steep hill over and over again. "Do we send the cavalry up again, General Abdul?"

Abdul was frustrated. Never had his cavalry – or any cavalry for that matter - been repelled repeatedly by infantry. "What do you want to do, General? Do you want to try another flanking manuever?"

"No." He peered up the mountain through his collapsable scope, trying to determine their numbers. "We don't know the size of their forces, nor how wide their position is on the mountain. The slope is steep. It could be a trap."

"Why don't we just march on to Tours. That will force them to come down from the mountain to defend their homes and families. Then we can choose the terrain to our advantage."

The proposal stung Abdul's pride all the more potently, given the common sense of the inferior's argument. He snarled at all the captains who nodded their heads in affirmation of the underling's proposal, perched on their feisty steeds. Abdul found it difficult to imagine accepting an option that looked too much like retreat. "No. Here is the enemy." He pointed up the mountain. "Shall I flee north? Shall the armies of Allah turn our tails and retreat? Absolutely not!" He shook his head side to side vigorously. "Send all the cavalry this time, full frontal assault." He collapsed the scope and handed it to an aid on horseback beside him.

"Including the reserves?"

"Yes, all of them. You! Mahmud!" Abdul pointed and shouted at another captain nearby. "Prepare the infantry to follow the cavalry up that hill. Our cavalry cannot do this many more times. We must break them right here with this charge."

* * * * *

The exhausted warriors who comprised the front lines of Martel's forces were ecstatic. They were doing what had never been done before. They were repelling armored cavalry – the best in the world – with inexperienced foot-soldiers! They shouted and chanted praise to God at the sight of so many slain Umayyad forces below them.

Martel gazed down the valley with his scope, studying the horde of warriors on the plain. "Oh no," he mumbled.

"What is it, Consul?"

"They're bringing them all. Even their infantry." Eighty thousand shouting Muslim warriors rushed toward them on horse and on foot.

"Can we stop them?"

Martel shut his telescope and raised his voice. "Pray men! Pray for God's help!"

"Sir John's attack on their camp was supposed to divide them, Consul."

Martel unsheathed his sword as his men shifted uneasily with their shields and spears. "It didn't work."

He called out to a messenger on horseback beside him in the densely packed defensive formation. "Relay this order. Have all forces drop down upon the Umayyad when they retreat this time."

* * * * *

"General Abdul!" One of the messengers rushed up to him on horseback with an urgent announcement. "General Abdul!"

The general became irritated at the interruption as he managed the huge assault up the mountain against an unknown number of enemy troops. "What is it?!"

"Our camp is being raided!"

"What?!" several warriors around the general shouted simultanously.

"A force emerged from the forest and caught us completely by surprise! The enemy has taken control of half of our tents and are freeing and arming our slaves..."

Several of General Abdul's chiefs and captains suddenly turned and began to gallop back toward the camp, taking many of their forces with them. They feared that they were being deprived of their wealth by the band of marauders.

General Abdul was furious! "No! Do not retreat! We must support our cavalry!" General Abdul screamed orders in vain. The only thing that the general's men feared more than their general's wrath was losing their wealth. One-fourth of his forces began to make their way toward camp as the rumor spread like wildfire. The others soon lost their vigor as their numbers thinned.

* * * * *

Charles Martel's impenetrable phalanx formation repelled the final massive cavalry charge. Drenched with sweat, cradling wounds, and gasping for air, they cheered ecstatically nonetheless.

Seeing that the Muslim forces had diminished and were in disarray, Martel finally gave the order for which his militia forces had so patiently waited. He thrust his sword into the air and his men quieted to give heed to his soul-stirring refrain. "For your wives!" he shouted. "For your children! For your posterity! For freedom and for King Jesus! Charge!"

The remainder of the battle was a slaughter, as the Christian troops pursued and decimated almost the entire Umayyad army. Abdul was slain in the descent of Charles Martel's forces down the mountain.

With a force of thirty thousand lay-warriors, Charles Martel had slammed the door of Europe on the more powerful and experienced Muslim army of eighty thousand, and had suffered only 1,500 casualties. Europe would remain Christian.

For a while.

* * * * *

Charity, Anna, and James were exhausted from dodging fleeing Muslims and sprinting in and out of abandoned tents across the plain, looking for Daniel.

"There he is!" James, panting heavily, pointed to a long horse carriage with bars as walls.

Two young Arabs tied the slave carriage to a train of horses. As they saw the white army move nearer, they grew nervous and hasty. They were easily disarmed and put to flight by Charity's arrows and the swords in the hands of James and Anna.

"James!" With his hands on the bars of his cage, Daniel bounced up and down with glee. "Charity! Anna! You found me!" The captive children around Daniel stood to their feet and gave thanks to

God for their rescuers.

"Are you all right?" Anna grabbed Daniel's hands through the bars.

"I am starving – we all are. You've missed some good church in this little jail cell though. We had revival!"

"Cal Zastrow would be proud." Charity grinned from ear to ear at her little brother's beaming enthusiasm. "Maybe Brother Cal will put one of your quotes in his little black book of martyrs' quotes."

"That'd be cool!"

James pulled at the immovable iron bars. "How can we get you out of here?"

"I haven't seen the guy all day who has the key to this cell."

Charity studied the corners of the jail cell. The walls were welded at each corner. "Everybody!" she said, addressing the children who packed the small cell. "I want you to lurch back and forth in there. Run side to side, all together. We're going to tip it over."

"Tip it over?"

"It's the only way we can free you. Now everybody run to me and lunge against the wall of the cage, and then run toward James and throw yourself against that wall." Charity pointed at James on the other side of the carriage.

The children lurched back and forth against the walls, finding the activity entertaining. The carriage began to tip each time they thrust their bodies against the side of the jail-cell-on-wheels.

"Keep doing it!" said James. He waved Charity and Anna over to him. "When they run to that wall again, help me push it over."

The carriage tipped on two wheels, and they lifted the side that was up in the air with all their might. They grunted and their faces contorted as they tried to tip the carriage all the way over until, finally, it crashed on its side. The bars popped out of their base where they connected to the wooden horse carriage, and everyone managed to squeeze out through the crack. The children all cheered, thanked God for deliverance, and congratulated each other.

"There you are." Sir John trotted his horse directly up to Charity. "You're not going to believe this, but I found your arrow."

"Where?"

He pointed southward. "There's a large square-shaped ditch

over there with hundreds of dead bodies in it. You'll find that Muslim captain with the orange hat right there in the middle of the pile."

"Did you see the arrow sticking out of his left side? Did it have bright yellow-green feathers at the tip?"

"No, but I haven't seen many orange-capped warriors since we've been fighting. It's got to be the one. Tell me, why do you need it so badly?"

"We can't get home without it. It's special." Charity grasped her bow with her left hand and grabbed Daniel's hand with her right and began to run in the direction Sir John pointed. "Come on! Hurry!"

"Godspeed!" He waved as his strange friends disappeared into the midst of a throng of white tents.

"Thank you, Sir John!"

* * * * *

When Charity, Anna, James, and Daniel arrived at the square-shaped pit that had been dug into the ground, they discovered that someone had already sprinkled oil on all of the bodies around the outer edge and set them afire.

"Oh no!" Charity mourned. "How can we get to it?"

"Here," said James. He set down the two swords he held in his hands and ran into a nearby tent. He grabbed the edge of a Persian rug that had covered the floor of the tent. "Help me with this. Let's lay this over the edge of the fire and then we can run across the flame."

When James pulled the carpet out of the tent, Charity set down her bow and bent to help him. Suddenly, a Muslim warrior hiding inside the tent charged right at James with a sword, trying to run him through the chest with a thrust of the blade.

"Ah!" James dropped the rug and dodged the first thrust, and then ducked the follow-up swing of the sword, but the warrior stepped on James' foot and snapped his anklebone like it was a rotten stick. James fell to the ground, screaming and rolling in excruciating pain. "Oowwww!"

The other Johnstons were frozen with fear until they heard the audible "snap" of James' anklebone. They startled as if shocked with an electrical wire. Writhing in pain, James grabbed his ankle and tried to roll away from the swordsman. The warrior raised his huge, thick scimitar into the air, preparing to bring it down upon James' head when Anna quickly lifted her sword to block it. But his sword was too heavy and sharp and it cut through hers like a razor blade through fishing string, sending half of Anna's blade flipping through the air where it stuck in the ground at an angle. James pulled it out of the dirt, and threw it at the Muslim warrior, slicing his cheek and sending him into an even greater rage. "Ah!" the bearded warrior screamed, preparing to take his vengeance with one mighty swing.

Charity was stiff with fear until it became obvious that her siblings were about to be slain before her eyes. Then she remembered the hatchet she had under her belt. Courage rose within in. She removed it and moved closer to defend her siblings.

Charity surprised even her own expectations. Her moves were effeminate and graceful, like a ballet dancer before a crowd of thousands, and yet terrifying and ugly all at the same time. In five swift, effortless moves, the bad guy was as dead as a rock on the moon, and Charity's skirt dripped with wet crimson. James, Daniel, and Anna were absolutely shocked at what they just witnessed. Even James forgot about his broken ankle and let out a yelp of praise at the sight of his sister's amazing exploit.

"Man! Charity, where'd you learn that?"

Charity ignored the question, and wiped her mouth with the back of her hand, breathing deeply with the hatchet resting in her sweaty grip.

"You were like Sampson with his donkey's jawbone," Daniel praised her.

Anna leaned over to James. "Are you okay, James?"

"Oh, it hurts," he said, standing to his feet with her help. "Ouch. I think I broke it. It's almost as bad as getting tickled."

"At least you didn't wet your pants," responded Anna. They all laughed as they recalled how terribly James hated being tickled.

"Come on," said Charity as she put her hatchet back under her belt. "We gotta hurry. The fire's spreading."

They dragged the carpet over to the edge of the pit and unrolled it over the dead bodies that burned at its edge. The fire was spreading inward fast.

"Let's go!" Daniel put his arm around James and helped him hobble over the bridge they had made over the fire. Their sisters followed them and just when the last person crossed it, the carpet began to burn. They struggled over the dead bodies to try to make their way to the warrior with the orange cap who lay on his belly in the center of the heap.

Charity began to dry heave. "Uh, the smell!" The bodies nearer the center had been there the longest and were stinking. Flies were buzzing everywhere. But the flames that slowly approached them from every side of the large square-shaped grave kept them motivated.

Charity reached the orange-capped Umayyad captain first and flipped him over. She gasped at the sight of him and let out a scream of horror.

"What is it?" Anna scrambled up the pile of bodies to stand beside Charity.

"It's not him! It's not him!" This warrior had a brown beard and had been killed with a sword to the neck, not an arrow.

"What are we going to do?" Anna cried out. "The fire's coming closer."

James tried to remain calm. "God's still on the throne. Let's pray."

"Right." said Daniel. "God can still save us."

Charity took the initiative and began to call out on the name of Jesus, with both of her hands raised to heaven. Before she even got three words out of her mouth, someone called out to them from the edge of the pit.

"Hey! Hey, over there!"

Charity stood on her tiptoes to see over the flames that rose to the sky all around them. "It's John!" Charity cupped her hands around her mouth and shouted, "It's the wrong guy!"

"I know! I'm sorry! But what in the world were you thinking? I found your arrow just as you described it in a dead captain over there!" He raised the arrow with the yellow and green feathers and pointed across the vast field of tents. "Get out of there! Run through the fire! Now!"

Charity's eyes began to well up with tears from the smoke. "We won't make it! We'll be burned to death."

Sir John glanced glumly at the foot soldier beside him. "They're going to be burned to death anyway."

"Got that right," the soldier responded. "What were they doing, running in there like that?"

Anna's eyes dripped more from grief than from the burning smoke. She felt the lowest she had ever felt in her life. She fell to her knees and tried to fight off the sob that swelled in her chest. She never missed her Mom and Dad more than she did right at this moment.

The young black-caped warrior waved at them from atop his steed. "I will see you in heaven, my brave friends!" The fire around the four Johnstons was closing fast, licking their shoes.

Charity cupped her hands around her mouth and projected her voice toward the young man. "Shoot the arrow at us!"

"What?"

"Shoot the arrow at us! It will save our lives!"

"How will it save your..."

"Just do it! Do it now!"

"But I could hit you with it!"

The foot soldier beside Sir John commented, "And how would that be bad?"

Sir John shrugged and whispered, "Good point."

Charity had to scream at the top of her voice to be heard over the roar of the flames: "Just do it!"

The young warrior beside Sir John pulled on his sleeve. "What's she saying? She wants you to shoot her?"

"Just give me your bow."

The young man handed Sir John his bow, and he aimed and shot the special arrow as best as he could right toward the center of the square, where the four Johnston children awaited their death.

The arrow landed five feet away from them in the center of a blaze of fire.

"Oh no!"

The four children huddled on the center of the back of the dead Muslim captain, the only place in the entire grave where the flames were not yet consuming flesh.

Charity stood to her feet and wiped her tears, which were caused more from the smoke than from grief. "Well, if we're all going to die in this flame anyway, at least I should be willing to endure it for ten seconds for the chance to save our lives." She handed James her bow and took a deep breath and prepared to jump into the flames.

"Wait!"

"I've got to try, James!"

James picked up a half-filled canteen of water at his feet. The metal was hot from being heated by the flames. He opened the cap and handed it to her. "Don't touch the bottom, it's getting warm. Your legs are still wet from hacking that bad guy with your hatchet, so drench your upper body with this water."

"What?" said Anna. "What are you going to do?"

Charity opened the canteen, poured the hot water over her head, neck, and arms, and then suddenly disappeared into the wall of flames that surrounded them. For five terrifying seconds, Anna, James, and Daniel heard and saw nothing but the raging flames.

"Charity!" They screamed for their sister through smoke-induced coughs. "Charity! Charity!"

Suddenly, her arm burst through the wall of flames and James brought the bow down to her so that it touched her hand. Anna and Daniel lunged to touch the bow and arrow and they all held their breath in silent prayer as the flames began to ignite their clothes and singe their hair.

It happened just as before. The flames that lurched at them suddenly exploded heavenward as if someone had thrown a thousand lit firecrackers at them. The heat that had begun to burn their extremities suddenly dissipated, and they felt the cool breeze of the spinning whirlwind. The whirlwind appeared to be made of the flames and debris from the warriors on which they stood, but they were not hot and smelly, but cool and aromatic. Anna looked at Charity's hand and saw that the flames no longer clung to it. They pulled Charity by the arm and lifted her through the wall of spinning flames into the center of the whirlwind. She came up to them with a painful grimace on her face.

"Oh, that was starting to hurt," she said. "Thank God for that canteen."

"And that it had water in it and not alcohol." James grinned at his own joke.

"Your hair's not even singed," Daniel noticed. Charity's flesh was as perfect as could be.

"My ankle doesn't hurt anymore either," James informed them. The four Johnstons hugged each other close as the whirlwind of flames began to speed up around them.

"God," Charity pleaded, "take us home. Please, take us home."

The whirlwind of flames gradually slowed and descended to the ground until they saw a clear, starry sky overhead and an early sunrise at the far end of a green field.

"We're not home," Charity mourned. "When is this going to end?"

The flames dissipated, leaving a circle of black and gray ash on the green grass where they stood near a dirt road full of potholes. A thick white fog hugged the ground tightly like a slab of melting butter on a pancake.

"Hey look! It's a rifle." Anna pointed at the weapon in Charity's right hand.

She looked at the butt of the gun, hoping to find the name "Johnny" scribbled therein. She saw no engraving. She studied the musket carefully and realized that it was both heavier and longer, and had a bayonet affixed to the end of it. It was not the same musket that they found beside the creek behind their home in Zanesville.

"What's that?" Daniel said. "Listen."

Before they realized what was happening, the distant rumble of marching feet somewhere in the dense fog became hundreds of British redcoats, running toward them in three columns.

"Hey!" A soldier shouted at the four children. "Get out of the way!"

The soldiers pushed Charity, Anna, and Daniel to their right, and James was shoved to the ground to the left of the columns.

"Interrogate those children," Major Pitcairn of the British force ordered.

Chapter 5

Major Pitcairn motioned to two soldiers, who immediately pulled out of line and grabbed James by an arm. Charity, Anna, and Daniel got on their feet and sprinted away before the soldiers could respond to his order.

"They could reveal our position and our numbers, Major. What do you want us to do?" A soldier joined several others in raising their rifles and taking aim at the fleeing children. "Do you want us to shoot?"

"They're children!" Major Pitcairn knocked the rifles down toward the ground with his sword.

"The tallest one there's armed, sir. They could be spies."

Major Pitcairn turned and saw that the eldest girl held a musket in her arms as she ran away toward a white house up the road. "Well, is she aiming it at you, private?"

"Not yet."

"You two!" Major Pitcairn pointed at two young soldiers. "Give chase. We need to find out what they know. If she doesn't lay down her weapon, then assume she's a spy. Find them and interrogate them."

"Yes sir." The soldiers sprinted into the fog in the direction that the three children ran.

Major Pitcairn began to question James in an attempt to discover whether this orange-headed boy knew if the militia had gotten wind of the British plan to sneak into Concord, Massachusetts and search for weapons reported to be stockpiled by the militia there.

"He says he's from Ohio," one of the soldiers holding fast to

James informed Major Pitcairn.

"Why won't y'all let me go?" James said, with a hint of worry in his voice.

"I'm Major Pitcairn. Are you a militia sympathizer?"

"A what?"

"Do you think that the American colonists have the right to govern themselves independently?"

James suddenly realized what was at stake. They had been dropped smack dab in the middle of a conflict between the British army and colonial militia. This had to be the Revolutionary War for American Independence.

"Answer quickly boy! Or you'll feel the edge of my sword against your palm." The men grabbing James' arms gave them a twist.

"Ow! No sir! I'm a British sympathizer!" James' heart dropped to his stomach. He had repented of dishonesty so many times that he had lost count, and here he was lying again. But he feared for his life. Was that a justification for lying? His countenance dropped and he began to stare at the ground in shame. His conscience was smitten. He should have told the truth or distracted them with a joke and not answered the question. Anything but a lie. He sensed the frown of God upon him, and his heart broke and eyes welled with tears. He knew that a little sin will spoil a lot of righteousness, and a little cowardice will ruin a lot of courage. To begin a race and not finish is worse than never beginning at all.

"Let him go." Pitcairn motioned at the two redcoats who did as they were commanded and let go of James. "Have you learned anything that might be of assistance to us?"

"No, I, uh..."

Pitcairn was growing impatient. He didn't let James finish his sentence, but turned and shouted at his men. "Double quick!" They began to quickly jog in sync up the road into the fog.

"Wait!" James called out to him, his heart pounding with conviction. He had lied to the British officer and he couldn't live with himself one more minute without confessing, even if it meant his death. "I'm not British! I'm American! Long live Mel Gibson! Wait—"

The soldiers ignored him, their breaths quickened and their ears were numb to all except the stomping of their feet against the dirt road, still damp from the night's mist.

James wasn't going to walk away from this moment with a guilty conscience. He began to run in the direction of the soldiers. "The South will rise again! The South will rise again!" He stopped, thought for a moment, and then realized that the chant his eldest sister frequently spouted during their games had no relevance to the Revolutionary War.

"Remember the Alamo!"

"The Alamo? What is that pest shouting about?" one soldier said to another with a shrug.

Then a light bulb went off in James' head. "No King but King Jesus!" James finally recalled the Revolutionary War motto as he jogged beside the troops. "No King but King Jesus!"

American colonialists were sticking their heads out of their windows and doors as the troops passed, and some of them heard the little orange-headed boy's memorable chant. One of them was a first term congressman who would propose the phrase "No King but King Jesus!" to be the official motto of the Revolutionary War.

"What!" Major Pitcairn became furious when he heard James' shout over the smacking of his troops' boots against the dust. "Halt! Who's saying that?"

"That orange-headed trouble-maker with the Old Navy shirt." The soldier pointed at James.

Major Pitcairn stepped through the three columns of soldiers and began to stomp up to the child who was quickly becoming a thorn in his side. "The redcoats are gonna lose!" James shouted as the British Major neared. "King George is a tyrant! You redcoats are gonna lose!" He refused to be intimidated at the Major's enraged snarl. The Major unsheathed his sword and James responded with a song. "God bless America," he sang at the top of his voice, unfortunately in a key that was too high for him, "land that I love! Stand beside her ..."

"Take that mad rebel into custody." Major Pitcairn pointed at the boy with his sword.

"...And guide her, with the bite from the light from above!" (James never was exactly sure of the words in that line of the song.) "From the mountains! To the prairies..." James continued to sing as they tied his hands behind his back. "To the ocean, white with foam!

God bless America! My home sweet home! God bless…"

"And shut him up before he wakes up the whole neighborhood." The soldier grit his teeth in anger and wielded the butt of his musket against the head of the colonial squirt. *Whack!* The blow knocked him unconscious.

* * * * *

Charity, Anna, and Daniel ran the opposite direction of the sunrise on the dirt road until they could no longer hear or see the columns of British regulars behind them through the dense fog. "James!" Anna screamed. "I thought he was behind us. Where—"

Charity put her index finger over her lips. "Shhh!"

Anna whispered back: "We can't just leave him."

"What's today's date?"

Anna shrugged. "I don't exactly have my calendar on me right at this moment."

"They're coming." Daniel's right ear was tilted in the direction from which they came. "I hear footsteps coming right at us."

They quieted and listened carefully for whatever it was that Daniel's keen ears heard through the dense fog. Two British soldiers suddenly burst out of the mist right in front of them. "There they are!" With one hand gripping his musket, one of the soldiers reached for the nearest child, who was Daniel.

Daniel instinctively ducked under the grasp of the redcoat who lunged for him.

Anna was quick. She delivered a well-placed karate strike of the index and middle fingers to the right eyeball of the soldier that reached for Daniel. "Taste my shuto!"

"Ow!" The soldier dropped his rifle and reached for his eyes with both hands.

The other soldier was furious at the audacity of these children to resist their government's soldiers. "Come here, you little rascal!"

Anna grabbed Daniel's hand and pulled him out of the range of the soldier's reach just as Charity raised her musket, pointed it at the soldiers, and cocked it. "Freeze! Put your musket down, now."

"What are you doing Charity?" Anna placed her palm on her

sister's shoulder. "You know you don't have–"

"Quiet!" Charity ordered Anna without looking at her. Anna almost gave away the secret that she didn't have a bullet in the gun. "You soldiers leave us alone."

"Little Missie, you don't know what you're doing." The soldier lowered his weapon and carefully placed it on the ground. The red-coat that had been poked in the eye was still moaning in pain. "Even aiming a weapon at a British regular is punishable by a thousand lashes of a whip. You'd beg for death, little g—"

"I said quiet!" Charity's blue eyes blazed like lasers down the barrel at the British soldier who stood with his hands up in the air. "Give me nothing to lose and I'd just as soon shoot you. Get on your knees. Put your hands in the air."

"Easy, easy, girl–"

"Do it! Now!" They instantly complied. "Has the war started?"

"What? What war?"

"The War for American Independence? Have the colonists rebelled?"

"I don't know what you're talking about."

"Where are we?"

"Lexington."

"Where are your fellow soldiers headed?"

"Uh, well, the king's business is not yours."

"Answer me! Or my sister will put her knife in your eye. Anna?"

"What?" Anna appeared surprised that Charity was singling her out.

"Open your pocketknife and poke his left eye out."

She opened her pocketknife with a mischievous grin and the soldier became nervous. "All right, all right. We're going to Concord to destroy the local militia's stockpile of weapons."

"Is that it?"

"We have orders from General Gage to arrest Sam Adams and John Hancock."

Hearing the names of those famous American forefathers made her hair stand on end. But they were more than great Americans. They were husbands. They were fathers with children. They were godly leaders. Charity grit her teeth at the news of the treacherous plan to kidnap these two American patriots. "What crime have they committed?" The soldiers did not respond.

"Anna and Daniel. Tie them up."

They tied the two redcoats' hands and feet together, and then gagged them and tied them to a tree beside the road.

"We gotta go warn the militia." Charity began to run on the dirt road as fast as she could with the heavy musket as Daniel and Anna tried to keep up with the muskets, powder, and ammo they confiscated from the British soldiers.

"Don't we need to find James first?" Daniel asked.

"If the soldiers let him go, he's okay. If they captured him, then finding the militia will be our best chance of getting him back. The militia must be warned so that they can hide their weapons and Hancock and Sam Adams can flee to safety before the redcoats arrive. I know that's why God brought us here. I just know it." The fog was just beginning to lift, and she could see that they were right next to a triangular-shaped field of grass.

The three darted into a restaurant that was just opening up for breakfast. A sign on the door read, "Buckman Tavern."

When they entered, Charity thought the room seemed more like an attic than a restaurant. Wooden beams criss-crossed the ceiling above them, and the room smelled musty and moldy. Oil lamps hung on the walls gave the room an eerie glow. In this early dawn hour, the room was already filled with men, young and old. Even more surprisingly, some of them were carrying long rifles.

Charity walked up to the oldest man who was nearest the door. "Do you know anyone in the militia who lives near here? I need to speak to them immediately."

"Well, we all are in the militia, little miss."

"Who's in charge?"

A lumpy man with a gravelly-voice stepped forward. "I am." He was the most formally dressed of the men, and had a pistol in a holster on his hip. "I'm Captain John Parker."

John! the Johnstons all thought at the same time, wondering if this would be the John that would get them all home.

"What's a little lady like you doing in Buckman Tavern with a musket at this time of day?"

"The British are coming."

Captain Parker's eyes widened and his back straightened. He

instinctively put his hand on his sword that hung sheathed at his waist. "What?"

"We ran into three columns of redcoats just east of here. They are headed to Concord to confiscate militia weapons. They've got word of a stockpile you're hiding there."

"Militia weapons?" Several of the men began to gather around, sharing anxious glances but gripping their muskets with determination.

One of the older men in the room ventured a rhetorical question. "Wonder how they learned about that?"

"Tory spies," another man responded halfway through a sigh.

Captain Parker studied the three young children for a moment, noting their unusual attire. "I don't believe you."

Daniel stepped in front of his sisters and raised his voice. "Our brother was probably kidnapped by them. We are telling you the truth!"

In behind the three Johnstons suddenly burst an unshaven wiry fellow who brushed the kids aside and walked right up to the man who was speaking with Charity. "Captain Parker! They are coming. I need one more rider. We've got to alarm the militia in every direction, and quick!"

"Told ya!" Charity snapped, glaring at the captain for his reluctance to believe her initial report.

Captain Parker reached for his pistol. "From where?" He checked and loaded his Colt as the wiry fellow answered.

"The Bay. Hurry! I need a rider now." He glanced around the room as if expecting someone to volunteer. "One of my express riders has the pox and can't make the journey."

"I need every shooter we have. I can't loan you a man. But you must make sure Concord is warned. The Brits are headed there to take possession of our hidden stockpile."

"And arrest Sam Adams and John Hancock," Daniel added. "Sam Adams won't get arrested though. He turns out to be President. I don't know much about Hancock, except that he signed the Declaration of—"

"What?"

"Never mind him," said Charity, giving Daniel a critical stare. Daniel didn't realize that the Declaration of Independence hadn't even been written yet.

"You young'uns are out of your minds."

"No, we're not. The Brits are headed to Concord to arrest Adams and Hancock. Those were Gage's orders according to a redcoat we—."

"I have to leave," the wiry express rider interrupted. "I'll make sure that Concord is warned, but I need another rider."

"Can't help you, Paul." Captain Parker ignored the express rider's plight and rallied his boys. "Breakfast is over, men. Let's make for the green." The Minutemen grabbed their gear and headed for the door.

Anna stepped forward. "I'll ride. I have a horse at home. I'm light and can ride fast."

"Do you know the road?"

"Just point me in the right direction. It's not like there's going to be a lot of confusing street signs and blinking yellow lights between here and the next town."

"Huh?"

Charity and Anna shared a glance and a grin, and Charity spoke to the horse-rider. "She can do it."

"All right. Follow me."

Charity watched as Anna followed the wiry express rider toward the door. Charity suddenly had a dreadful feeling in her gut, like the feeling you get when you are in an airplane and sudden turbulence pushes you down and prompts you to look out the window to make sure you are still level. Something just didn't feel right. She was losing her bearings. Things were happening too fast. Were they being too hasty in entering this conflict? This wasn't their war. This wasn't even their century. However, this was their country, and God sent them here for some unknown reason. She knew that if they didn't discover it, they'd never make it home. If home was their Promised Land, then this trip through time was their wilderness. If they weren't faithful in the wilderness, would they ever cross the Jordan? Was there a way home without taking up the burden of the oppressed colonists? She didn't think so. At least now they were in America, much closer to home than they were in Israel or in eastern Europe. She released her burden to God and received an instantaneous peace that everything would be okay.

"Anna!" Anna stopped at the door and turned to face her big sister. "Where are we going to find you when this is over?"

"Don't worry." The big smile on Anna's face put Charity at ease. "I'll find you. I'll be riding a horse. Hyah!" She hailed her sister with her right fist thrust into the air, and then leaped through the doorway, following the skinny fellow into the yard.

Charity returned the hearty farewell. "Hyah!"

Anna followed the rider to two horses that were tied up to a post on the side of the Buckman Tavern. "Where am I going?"

"We've got men going every direction, but this horse is very familiar with the rough road to Concord." He patted the brown mare that Anna was going to ride. "So I want you to go to Concord. Can you remember what you're supposed to do when you get there?"

"Yes. Tell the militia to hide the stockpile and warn Adams and Hancock. Got it."

The skinny man took his triangular-shaped hat off and pointed west down the dirt road. "Concord is twenty-some-odd miles that way. Just shout at every home you pass, 'The British are coming!' They'll know what to do."

As he instructed Anna, she stroked the mane of the huge quarter horse. It stood taller than Taffy, her paint mare at home, and didn't have the temper or the physique of a pampered pet. It was a tall, lean beast, who snorted and stomped as she caressed it. She tightened the stirrups and nodded at the express rider's counsel. She hopped into the saddle effortlessly, and then bent low to whisper softly into the horse's ear.

Her affection for the beast caused the mare to neigh and the express rider to smile. "What's your name, little horse master?"

"Anna."

"I'm Paul Revere." He mounted his own steed and Anna gazed at him in wonder. "God speed you on your journey. Stop for nothing and no one. Our liberty may depend on it."

"What's my horse's name?"

"Princess."

This was a dream come true!

* * * * *

To the rhythm of the drummer boy's tapping, Captain Parker rushed his men out of Buckman Tavern into the triangular-shaped grassy field in front of it. They formed a line on the north side of the field, so as to face the oncoming British regulars. The cross on the church steeple cast a long shadow across the field as the fog lifted.

"Stand your ground," Captain Parker ordered the Minutemen as he paced back and forth behind them. "Do not fire unless fired upon. But if they want to have a war, let it begin here." The captain's gravelly voice echoed across the green, arousing many from the comfort of their beds in downtown Lexington. Many patriots awakened to the harsh reality of the inevitable conflict, and they fell to their knees in prayer for their leaders, for their people, and for their freedom.

A young civilian in fancy clothes turned to Charity and asked her, "Where are you kids from?"

"From Ohio."

"Militia from Ohio? What in the blazes are you doing out here?"

"Oh, we're just visiting." Charity began to carefully load her musket, so glad that she had just studied muskets in home school. She explained each step of the process to Daniel, who loaded his. "It kicks a lot harder than the 22 you're used to shootin', so make sure the butt of the rifle is deep in the pocket of your shoulder." Daniel nodded excitedly, his teeth firmly gripping his bottom lip.

The young man beside them continued to watch and listen to Charity as she instructed Daniel. Daniel saw him observing them and said, "We aren't real militia. We just want to help y'all."

The young man had a confused look on his face. "Around these parts, a kid with a musket defending his God-given rights *is* militia."

The church bells began ringing across the green. Citizens all around them watched the scene unfold from their second-story windows. Some were brave enough to observe from the dirt roads on each side of the green.

Captain Parker raised his voice and brought his men to attention. "Here they come."

The redcoats moved from the road onto the green and the Minutemen could now see them clearly. Captain Parker let out a disturbing grunt that made the fellows around him glance back at him nervously. There were several hundred British soldiers heading straight toward them on the double.

Charity saw the young man beside her put his tri-cornered hat on the ground in front of him and fill it with musket balls. He kept looking over his shoulder at a house beside the road.

"What are you looking at?"

"That's my home." He pointed back at a two-story house beside the road. "That's my brand new wife looking at me through the second floor window."

Charity saw the young pretty lady with her head out of the window of a white house, and she waved at her. The woman waved back and Charity felt compassion for the newly married couple. "What's your name?"

"Jonathan Harrington."

Her eyes widened. *Could this be the Johnny that gets them home?*

"You know, in Bible times, newly married men wouldn't have to go to war for a year. Why don't you go home to your wife?"

Jonathan smiled. "She just might be pregnant with my baby, ma'am. Shouldn't I be willing to sacrifice my life for my child to be free? The British treat colonists like animals. I'm not accepting that for my children. They will be free or their papa will die trying to make them free."

Captain Parker's gravelly voice suddenly broke the uneasy silence. "Disperse you men! Do not fire. Disperse!"

"What?" Jonathan was not pleased at all with this order. "I resolved never to run from the British, Captain."

"Just gonna find some more militia to stand with us, son. It's pointless to fight here. There's too many of them. Let's beat them back to Concord."

The militia turned and began to scatter. When the British soldiers caught sight of the rebels leaving the Lexington green with their muskets, they became enraged that these colonial rats would dare consider opposing them at all. Throwing tea into the bay to protest taxes was one thing, but presuming to bring your musket to a field of battle across from British soldiers is quite another. The redcoats broke ranks and began to charge the green.

Major Pitcairn tried to get his British regulars under control. "Do not fire! Keep your ranks." He shouted at the Minutemen, "Throw down your arms, you rebels, and you'll come to no harm!"

* * * * *

As Charity followed her new friend Jonathan off the green, she looked in the direction down the road where she had tied up the two soldiers, and she saw that they had somehow loosed themselves. One of them was aiming a musket he had confiscated from a civilian right at them. He was closer to them than the band of British regulars and was aiming his weapon right at Captain John Parker.

"Captain Parker! Get down! A sniper!"

"What?" Captain Parker and Jonathan Harrington said simultaneously.

Charity laid down flat, took careful aim at the soldier, and gently squeezed the trigger.

Blam!

The "shot heard around the world" had been fired. A vengeful British private entered eternity, and Captain John Parker's life had been saved.

Two or three nervous shots followed, with confused shouts of "Fire!" and "Hold your fire!" The Minutemen ducked the poorly aimed musket balls that whizzed erratically over their heads. Finally, a British officer organized his troops to give a unified volley at the Minutemen forces across the green, but not one Minuteman had been hit.

"Everybody all right?" Captain Parker called out to the anxious but determined militia forces. These farmers were facing off with the fastest and strongest of the British expeditionary forces, and they were vastly outnumbered.

"Throw down your arms!" Major Pitcairn ordered. "Why don't you rebels lay down your arms?"

As if in answer to the question, several Minutemen formed a line, took careful aim, and fired a volley at the British. As they reloaded, the British fired their second volley, tearing into the colonists. Jonathan Harrington, who stood beside Charity, fell to the ground clutching his chest. She could hear the man's wife call out his name from her second floor balcony across the street. He crawled off the green as Charity ducked speeding musket balls. Then he gradually rose to his feet and stumbled toward his front door.

Charity finished reloading, put her musket over her shoulder, and rushed to help Jonathan across the dirt lane. "Daniel, let's help him home." She and Daniel got on each side of the young man and supported him as he staggered up the stairs that led to his front door.

"I'm sorry," Charity said when he began to cough up blood. "I'm so sorry."

The man moaned in agony, his face gradually turning a pale white. When they reached the front door, he began to gasp for air. His weeping wife opened the door and he fell to the ground and stretched his hands toward her. He closed his eyes and breathed his last the moment she knelt down before him. Charity and Daniel began to cry as they watched her grieve. She laid her body across him, put her rosy cheek up against his clammy white cheek, and wept. The Harrington family was paying the cost of freedom.

Charity looked back and saw several other Minutemen get shot in another round of firing. The charging British infantry ran through the survivors with the bayonets affixed to their muskets. The main body of British soldiers gave three shouts of "Huzzah!" as most of the Minutemen on the green were now dead or dying. The British re-organized and began their march to Concord.

* * * * *

"British soldiers are coming! To arms!" Anna shouted at the top of her voice as she passed homes on the way to Concord. "The British are headed to Concord!" Her horse was covered with sweat, and did not even slow for those who gathered at the edge of the road to hear her message. "The British are coming! Your war for independence has begun!"

All over Massachusetts, hundreds of fathers, husbands, and sons kissed their families goodbye, and hastily packed food, muskets, ammo, and plenty of gunpowder. The Massachusetts militia answered the call to fight for their freedom. They began their historic journey toward Concord on the heels of the express riders.

* * * * *

When Anna finally reached the city limits of Concord, she stopped at the driveway of a brown-bearded man who carried a musket over one shoulder and a stringer of three ducks over the other. He instructed his boys to bring Anna and her horse some water.

"Are you sure that the British are coming?" he asked.

Anna nodded. She only took a sip of water, and then exclaimed hurriedly, "I need to speak to whoever's in charge of the militia! It's a matter of great urgency, sir."

"Well, you've come to the right place. I'm corporal of the Concord militia." He set the butt of his heavy musket on the ground.

Anna dismounted and shook the man's hand. "Captain John Parker and Paul Revere sent me to tell you that the British intend to raid the stockpiles of weapons that you have stored here in Concord."

The man's eyes grew wide. "What?"

"They know about your stockpile. Spies have ratted you out. You must re-locate your weapons. Or better yet, load them and put them into capable hands to fight. The British are headin' this way."

There was a hint of fear in the eyes of the militia leader, followed by a gritty determination to walk this road to the very bitter end. He clenched even tighter to his well-worn musket as he glanced worriedly at his three teenage boys.

The eldest of the three boys asked, "Do you want us to fetch our guns, father?"

He nodded soberly, and the three rushed toward the house.

"Don't worry," Anna encouraged him with a smile. "You'll win this war. God'll see you through to freedom."

The man took Anna's ladle, dipped it in the bucket of water the horse was drinking, and then he drank it down. "Losing the war is not what worries me." He wiped his beard with the back of his hand. "What concerns me is that I'll lose my boys to win it."

Anna shook her head back and forth. "Losing your life to win freedom for your posterity isn't a loss; in heaven's eyes, it's victory."

* * * * *

The tearful Mrs. Harrington gestured Daniel and Charity inside her home to avoid getting shot by the straggling redcoats in the streets. They dragged her husband into the foyer by his hands, and she put a blanket over his body.

Charity peeked out of the window at the British troops that passed the house. "What are we going to do, Daniel? How are we going to find James and Anna?"

"I don't know where James is. But I know Anna's heading to Concord. Let's follow the soldiers there, from a distance."

Charity and Daniel joined a growing throng of armed men, young and old, who followed the body of seven hundred British soldiers at a distance, careful to stay out of sight. Soon, Captain John Parker joined their contingent with many more militia. Sam Adams, John Hancock, and the pulpits of Massachusetts' churches had set brushfires of liberty in the hearts and minds of the people, and they were ready to lay down their lives for the chance to be free.

* * * * *

When the British troops reached Concord, they discovered that almost all of the powder, cannon, and muskets had been moved and hidden elsewhere. Tory spies gave the officers alternative locations and the Brits broke up into smaller groups and led search parties in different directions. A hundred British soldiers had been left at North Bridge, which was nothing more than a cluster of homes on a dirt road just north of Concord. A group of militia that had been shadowing the British forces took this opportunity to engage them.

When the British soldiers saw three hundred militiamen – and one militia-girl – making their way toward North Bridge, they panicked. They had been separated from their main force and were vulnerable. They fired first and dropped several Minutemen. The militia fired in return and four redcoats fell to the ground with fatal wounds.

The British soldiers were shocked. These rebels did not flee as those on the Lexington Green had done. They stood their ground and calmly aimed. As the British leveled their sites at them, the militiamen calmly reloaded. The colonists were willing to risk their lives to win their freedom, whereas many of these British soldiers were not as willing to risk their lives to take it away. Many of the redcoats turned and ran back to Concord, and when those who stood their ground against the Minutemen saw that their numbers were dwindling, they too turned and ran.

"They're running!" Charity led them in the cheer she found so contagious. "Huzzah!"

"Huzzah!"

"What should we do?" someone asked.

All eyes were fastened on Captain Parker, who seemed to be at a loss for words on what to do next.

The sad image of Jonathan Harrington's death in the arms of his young bride was firmly etched in Charity's mind. Mixed with the adrenaline rush of being shot at during the birth pangs of her nation, her whole body trembled. There were no words for the emotions she felt radiating from her heart. This conflict was personal now. Charity stood to her feet and thrust her musket into the air, red-faced, shouting through her tears, "They're in our country! They're the invaders! Let's chase 'em out!"

"Huzzah!"

* * * * *

The British search parties fled to Concord to re-group. The officers then decided to march their men to Charleston and join with reinforcements. They didn't plan on small groups of militia making target practice of them every step of the way.

The redcoats were frustrated; colonists hid behind houses, trees, and bridges, and picked them off one by one. Even the horses were shot out from underneath their officers.

The British officers sent out flankers to try and flush the woods of militia snipers, but the flankers soon became exhausted from trying to travel through the brush at the same frantic pace as the main body of troops on the road. They soon fell behind and became victims themselves.

A flanker came close to their position beside a creek, and he was taking aim at Charity who was in the process of reloading. Daniel saw him and leveled his gun at him.

Blam!

Charity looked back and saw Daniel recover from the recoil and then smile at her. "Good shot, Daniel!"

"I saved your life with that one."

"Thanks."

Daniel rubbed his bruised shoulder for a moment. "These muskets sure do kick hard."

"Come on." Charity jumped out of the creek bed and ran up ahead. "We gotta keep moving to keep ahead of them."

"Spread yourselves out!" Captain Parker ordered the militia to shadow the British who had fled back toward the Bay. "Reload as you re-position yourselves. Keep up the heat. Make them wish they'd never set foot in Massachusetts!"

Even when what remained of the exhausted British force finally joined with reinforcements, the militia gunfire continued to inflict casualties against them.

The British lost two hundred and fifty soldiers to death or injury, while the American militia only lost a hundred. They had beaten the British in the first day of eight years of war that would conclude with the birth of the United States of America.

While the militia celebrated their victory in the Buckman Tavern, Sam Adams walked into the room through a back door. Everyone who saw him shouted, "Huzzah!" and hoisted their drinks into the air. Charity and Daniel joined in, raising their steaming cups of cinnamon apple cider. Sam Adams smiled and waved at the enthusiastic greeting. The crowd quieted themselves and the father of the American Revolution raised his voice to address them. "We have this day begun to restore the Sovereign to Whom all men ought to be obedient. God reigns and from the rising to the setting of the sun, let His kingdom come..."

As he spoke, Charity thought this famous politician sounded more like a preacher. Then she recalled that in the early days of our nation's history, politicians were preachers, and the nation's pulpits were their podiums. There was no separation of church and state at the birth of America.

"Contemplate the mangled bodies of your countrymen, and then ask what should be the reward of such sacrifices? Our dead countrymen bid us to resist the dogs of war who have been let loose on us to riot in our blood and hunt us from the face of the earth..."

Charity and Daniel's thoughts went to Jonathan Harrington and all of the young Americans who had lost their lives today. *If we only had more fighters,* thought Charity, *maybe we could have stopped them on the green before they ever got to Concord.* The next words of Sam Adams were a reproof to her thoughts.

"If ye love wealth better than liberty, the tranquility of servitude more than the animated contest of freedom, go from us in peace. We ask not your counsels or arms. Crouch down and lick the hands that feed you. May your chains sit lightly upon you, and may posterity forget that you were our countrymen. But if you would have liberty, know this: victory goes not to the mighty, but to the righteous. Virtue is the seed that will grow into the fruit of a new nation. Sin will more surely overthrow the liberties of America more than the whole force of the enemy. While the people are virtuous they cannot be subdued; but when once they lose their virtue they will be ready to surrender their liberties to the first invader."

Charity and Daniel looked at each other, their mind buzzing with the revelation. "Did you catch that?" Charity asked Daniel.

Daniel blinked. "I think so." These were big thoughts for a seven-year-old.

"It's righteousness that brings freedom, Daniel. Not numbers. Not military power. Because righteousness brings the blessings of God, and freedom is one of the most precious of God's blessings."

Charity found herself gripping her musket tighter as he spoke. Today's conflict was her conflict, but this war was not her war. She was a visitor in their fight. But she knew that God wanted her to remember what happened to her today, what she heard, what she felt, and what happened to Jonathan Harrington and his lovely wife. She lived in a different generation with different tyrants to face and different weapons to wield, but these lessons applied in every age. The conflict between sin in government and righteousness in government, between tyranny and freedom was ever raging. No generation was exempt from the need for righteousness and vigilance to remain free. The liberty of her children and her children's children would depend upon the righteousness of her generation, the salti-ness of the salt of the earth. The words of the famed Sam Adams echoed in her mind: "While the people are virtuous they cannot be subdued."

Her thoughts were interrupted when Paul Revere burst through the front door.

An inharmonious chorus of "Huzzah!" rang out at the sight of the famed express rider who rallied the militia to Concord that day.

He hardly acknowledged the praise when he quickly approached Charity and Daniel. "I have news regarding your brother and your sister."

"James and Anna?" Charity's heart skipped a beat at the thought that Revere was about to make a terrifying announcement. "Are they okay?"

Paul Revere sighed deeply. "We discovered the whereabouts of your brother James. He and other captured militia are being held at a British prison near the Bay. The location's guarded by British gun-ships just off shore. Your brother admitted that he would fight the British if freed, so he's due to be executed as a traitor by tomorrow morning."

Charity and Daniel shared a startled glance. "What?" Charity was stunned. "That can't be. He's only eight!"

"There have always been sons of liberty that young among us. The redcoats will have no mercy on him."

Daniel couldn't believe his ears. "They're gonna execute James?"

"Yes. So Anna went to see what she could do to free him."

"All by herself?" Charity put her hand over her mouth and fought the fear that quickened her pulse and made her mouth dry as chalk.

"I couldn't afford a man to assist her. It was too risky."

Daniel put his hand on his sister's shoulder to calm her. "What in the world can Anna do to free James from a British prison?"

Paul Revere answered the question. "I asked her the same thing, and you know what she said?"

"What?"

Tears welled up in the eyes of the famed express rider. "I can do all things through Christ who strengthens me." He sniffed back his emotion and massaged his whiskers, apparently moved by the courage of the young woman he barely knew. "She's proven herself capable of doing everything else that was impossible for her to do today. I've got an unction that God might use her to put the rest of us to shame."

Charity looked at Daniel with a gritty determination evident on her face. "We gotta go find her and help."

"I've got some horses I can loan you."

Charity picked up her musket. "Come on, Daniel."

Daniel grinned, grabbed his musket, and followed Charity toward the door. Captain John Parker stopped Charity and Daniel at the front door and bowed before them. "You two were indispensable to our victory. We thank you for your help, don't we boys?"

The men echoed their captain's sentiment with "Amens" and "Huzzahs".

"Godspeed," John Parker said as they followed Paul Revere from the Tavern. "We will keep you all in our prayers."

* * * * *

James had just prayed himself to sleep with four other condemned traitors in the filthy jail cell situated on the edge of a cliff overlooking the Bay. He became startled when he thought he heard a tap on the bars of the cell.

He sat up and studied his surroundings for a moment. He thought the sound of the waves crashing on the rocks was playing tricks on his mind. He settled back down on his flea-ridden bed of smelly hay when he heard the tapping again. He opened his eyes and heard the hushed whisper of his name: "James. James."

He sat up and looked at the window that faced the ocean. "Who is that?" The other militia began to stir in their uneasy sleep. "Shhh. It's me, Anna."

"Anna?" James made his way to the window, searching for her features in the moonlight. Anna was walking on a narrow ledge beside a cliff that dropped down to the ocean. She clung to the rocks mortared to the prison wall to steady her precarious position. By the light of the full moon, James could see three British gunships anchored just offshore. "If they see you," James said, motioning to the gunships, "they'll send word and have you captured, or else make target practice of you."

"I needed to be sure you were here before I rescued you."

"How are you gonna do that?"

"I've got a plan." She rubbed her finger against the mortar that affixed the bars on the window to the stone wall. She noticed it was dry and that it crumbled between her fingers. "This mortar's soft. I think it'll work."

"What?"

"Just get ready to come out through an opening I'm going to put right here." She unlatched a stretch of looped rope that hung on her hip. She tied one end through the bars twice, and then tied a strong knot.

"What are you going to do? Don't do anything dangerous."

"James, they are going to execute you in the morning. We'll never test the limits of our faith unless we're willing to step off the boat and onto the water."

"I think that's a figure of speech." He gazed at the waves crashing against the cliff fifty feet below the ledge where Anna stood. "That's not to be taken literally."

"Like Pastor Bounds said, 'How do you spell *faith?*'"

"R-I-S-K," James spelled out the word. "Is that knot going to hold?"

"Charity taught it to me, and you know her knots always hold." Anna walked the narrow ledge of the wall back from whence she came and whistled to her horse. The horse neighed softly and cantered to her from the shadows.

Anna tied the end of the rope around her waist, mounted the tall, muscular horse, and gave her a kick and a quiet "Hyah."

The horse took off until the rope became taut, and then it pulled Anna off the back of the horse!

"Ow." Anna moaned and held her pained stomach, and then laughed at herself for a moment as she lay on the ground to recuperate. "Okay," she mumbled, "let's try that again. Except this time use your brains."

This time, she tied the rope around the horse's saddle. But as she did so, she tried to imagine "using her brains" in a literal sense by tying the rope around her forehead. She ended up giggling so hard she could barely quiet herself. She mounted the horse and clicked her tongue in her mouth while gently tapping her with her heels. The horse was reluctant to obey this time, for fear of hurting her gentle rider. The horse neighed and Anna tried to quiet her: "Shhh. Quietly, Princess. There are soldiers in the front of this building who'd love to fill both of us full of holes. Come on!" She patted the horse's hind leg with her right hand and issued a soft, "Hyah."

To James, it felt as if the whole building suddenly lurched toward the cliff. The other prisoners awoke, worried that an earthquake would shake them over the precipice to their deaths on the jagged rocks below. But the trembling stopped, and they realized that the bars of the only window in the room were sucked out of their place in the wall. Now the whole neighborhood woke up with the crash!

The heavy iron bars and the iron frame dropped over the cliff, swung over to Anna's side of the building, and began to pull the horse sideways toward the ledge. The horse neighed loudly as it tried to keep its footing.

"Whoops." Anna unfolded her pocketknife and quickly cut the rope. "Sorry girl."

* * * * *

"Captain! Captain!" A sailor that stood on the bow of the ship nearest shore pointed to the prison on the edge of the cliff above them.

"What is that?" the ship's captain wondered, reaching to take the hand scope from the sailor. "A rock slide?"

"It's a breakout, Captain." The private handed him the scope and the captain looked for himself. "I can see a horse and a civilian rider just to the left of the prison by the light of the moon."

"I see them." He collapsed the scope and turned and shouted to his men, who were just rousing from their nightly game of cards to step out on deck and discover what their fellow sailors were shouting about. "Get your muskets, men. Come on! We can't let those traitors escape!"

* * * * *

James and the other patriots in his jail cell struggled to make their way through the hole in the wall, over the rubble, along the ledge facing the cliff, and out to freedom. The guards that slept in the front part of the prison thought an earthquake had shaken the city. When they checked on the prisoners and saw them escaping, they sounded the alarm and called the troops into action.

"Come on, James!" Anna hollered from on top of her horse as she reached down and helped him up.

"Anna! You're crazy!" James grabbed her hand and leapt up onto the horse's back.

A shrill "pop" sounded behind them as if a huge paddle had smacked against the ocean. Then right beside them, shards of stone exploded as a three-quarter inch musket ball collided with the prison wall. Several more bullets fired, and one of the militia that was escaping from the prison with James was struck by the second shot. He tumbled and fell over the cliff with a scream.

"They're firing at us! Hold on James! Hyah!" Anna ordered her horse full speed ahead.

Just as the horse reached full speed, the soldiers came around the corner carrying torches. "Prepare to fire!" An officer pointed at the pair fleeing on the huge horse and

several soldiers took aim. Just as they fired their first volley, James' grip on Anna's waist loosened and he fell, flipping backward off the hips of the horse.

"No!" Anna leapt from her horse just as the second row of soldiers fired a volley. The horse was struck and tumbled forward several times until it came to a stop somewhere in the darkness ahead of them.

"James! James!" Anna knelt beside James and was horrified to discover that he had been struck in the head with a musket round. She began to cry as she held his face in her hands. Her tears fell down her cheeks and landed onto his face as the bullets whizzed over their heads.

James opened his eyes and thought for a moment that no words were coming out of his sister's mouth. He watched her lips cry out his name by the light of the silver moon, but couldn't hear anything. Then he realized what was happening. He was going to heaven to be with Jesus. There was no pain, no fear, and no regrets. He basked in the most amazing calm he had ever experienced in his life.

"James!" Anna cried one more time before he closed his eyes. "Oh God, please let him live." She looked over her shoulder as the redcoats closed in around them, some aiming their muskets and others unsheathing their swords.

* * * * *

"What's that?" Daniel was startled when he heard the crash from the east in downtown Lexington. He and Charity had tied up the horse and were sneaking around town to try to discover the location of the British prison where the accused traitors were incarcerated.

Charity appeared frightened by the same crashing sound that had startled Daniel. She ducked down behind one of the bushes beside them. "I don't know, Daniel."

Daniel started trotting toward the bay. "Maybe it's Anna. Come on."

Charity jumped out from behind the cover of the bushes, grasping tightly to the special musket. They joined dozens of curious citizens who were headed toward the Bay to see what caused the thunderous crash. Soon, they heard gunshots coming from the same vicinity.

They entered a courtyard and saw four thick wooden posts standing ten feet out of the ground. Behind the courtyard was a grassy field with a stone wall at the far edge of the field. "What is that?" asked Daniel.

"That's where they shoot the condemned," a citizen who walked beside them said.

Charity looked at Daniel, her eyebrows raised with sincere concern. "That's where James is going to die in the morning unless we can stop it."

"Oh no. Make that James and Anna." They saw the guards leading Anna back toward the front entrance of the jail. Behind them, they dragged James by his feet. James did not move, and a trail of blood dribbled onto the cobblestone walkway from his head wound.

"James!" Daniel cried out. "Oh no, Charity. He's dead."

Charity saw one of James' hands grab the grass beside the stone sidewalk as he was dragged back to the prison, and the hope reflected in her voice: "He moved!" She grasped Daniel's arm excitedly. "His hand moved, Daniel. James is still alive."

Anna looked in the direction of Daniel's cry, but could not see him down the dark street through all of the citizens who had gathered to find out what had caused the loud crash that awakened them from their slumber. A soldier prodded her on from behind, and she almost lost her footing. The soldier grabbed her by the hair and thrust her through the doorway into the British prison.

"I think I've got a plan, Daniel," Charity quietly uttered.

Daniel saw the smirk of adventure in the face of his sister as she conspired and prayed silently for wisdom.

"This isn't one of your 'Rescue the slave' games, Charity. This is real."

"I know, Daniel. You have to trust me."

* * * * *

"Is he going to make it?" A British prison guard sitting behind a wooden desk motioned to the orange-headed prison escapee shackled in solitary.

"If he stops bleeding, he'll survive to his execution." The sly grins of the soldiers exhibited the cruelty that war breeds in warriors if they spurn the still, small voice of conscience.

Anna had been locked into a cell with the other prisoners. From where she was, she could only see the feet of her brother as he lay unconscious on the floor, shackled to a hook on the wall. "He needs a doctor!" Anna's shrill scream penetrated the humid air like an arrow. "Please! Help him!"

An unexpected knock at the door caused one of the four jittery British guards to draw his pistol. "Who is it?"

"Two more traitors."

The announcement of the young woman's sharp voice made the guards wince in confusion. "Huh?"

One of the guards went to the door, put his eye through the peephole and saw that the two children outside looked just like the two traitorous rascals they had inside. They did not appear to be armed. He opened the door and leaned against the side of the doorframe. "Is this some sort of joke?"

"Let our brother and sister go," Charity spouted at the redcoat through clenched teeth. Daniel stood beside her, his hands firmly clasped in front of him.

"Charity!" Anna called out. "Is that you?" Anna went to the bars of her cell and saw that Charity and Daniel were at the door. "What are you doing? Get out of here!"

"Just let them go," Charity said matter-of-factly, "and no harm will come to you."

The soldiers laughed at the confidence of the feisty redhead. "We'll let them go to their graves in the morning. How's that for your liking?"

Daniel suddenly reached behind his back and pulled a bayonet that had been tucked under his belt. He lunged for the soldier's stomach just as Charity released a front snap-kick into his groin, but the soldier was on guard and took a quick step back. The skilled British guard disarmed the boy and pushed the girl onto the ground. One soldier behind them raised his pistol and another unsheathed his sword.

"Please!" mocked the soldier. "You insult me with your pitiful treasonous attacks." The soldier pointed his sword at Charity. "Assaulting a British soldier is an assault on the king. Seize them."

* * * * *

At first dawn, the children awoke to the sound of the trumpet outside. James aroused from his unconsciousness and sat cross-legged on the ground, his wrist still chained to the wall. He had lost a lot of blood from the musket wound that made a long streak on the right side of his scalp, where it had grazed his skull. Charity and Daniel were in a third cell across from James, and Anna remained in the large cell with other condemned militia.

"James, you look so much better." Anna's voice was warm and comforting to them all. Charity and Daniel came to the door of their cell so they could see Anna. "I thought you were dead last night, James."

James took a deep breath. "No, not yet. Charity, how did you and Daniel wind up in here?"

Charity hung her head in shame. "We tried to break you out."

James sighed. "And now we're all going to see the Lord today."

"I don't know." Charity had a tinge of hope in her voice. "The Lord may yet deliver us."

"Yeah." Daniel nodded at James. "God is a God of miracles, right?"

One British soldier had remained at attention in the room throughout the night. When the trumpet sounded, he sat down and relaxed while the other British soldier in the room who slept on a cot awakened and walked over to James' cell. Two soldiers who had been standing at attention just outside of the front door stepped inside, happy to conclude their night shift guard duties.

"There will be no deliverance for any of you." The British soldier removed a key from his pocket, opened James' cell door and unshackled him. Then he opened the doors of the other cells, bringing the other three Johnstons out to stand in a line while another soldier shackled their hands behind their back. Another soldier removed their shoes while the fourth soldier kept guard with his pistol at the ready.

Anna saw James' body wobbling back and forth. There were hardened streams of blood down the right side of his head and neck. His hair was matted with it. The right side of his shirt was stained maroon and stiff from the dried blood. "You all right, James?"

James' eyes dimmed. "I'm dizzy."

The door was opened and they were shoved toward the exit. One of the militia that remained in Anna's cell bade her farewell. "I shall pray for you. And I'll see you in heaven."

Anna turned and smiled as she exited the room. "Pray for the United States of America."

"For who?"

"For your country. That'll be the name of your country when you win your independence."

As they were led to their place of execution, James began to pray out loud. "Dear God, give our country freedom. Rid us of tyranny. Let Your kingdom come here. Let our enemies be drawn to You through our bravery."

Four redcoats stepped out of nearby barracks and stood at attention with their backs to the prison wall. They loaded their muskets about twenty yards away from the four thick wooden posts that stuck out of the ground. The soldiers that led the Johnstons out of the prison tied each prisoner to a post, and then they marched in a single file line to join the four other soldiers in preparation for the military execution. The children were speechless as they watched their executioners cruelly prepare the instruments of death. Their breath quickened as the superior officer gave orders to the row of soldiers.

"Daniel, it's time."

The captain glanced up at the sound of Charity's urgent whisper, but returned his attention to his men. Charity began to dig into the ground with her toes. Daniel did the same. "James, Anna, do what I'm doing."

"What?"

"Do it."

"James. James!" Charity, who was at one end of the line, raised her voice at her younger brother, who was at the other end. He appeared to have either fallen asleep or drifted into unconsciousness. "James! Wake up James!"

"Stop freaking out. Why are you screaming?" At a time like this, Anna didn't think Charity's extreme concern about James' sleepiness was necessary. "He lost a lot of blood last night. Let him be. Short of a miracle, we're all about to meet Jesus anyway."

"Wake up James!" Charity screamed even louder.

Daniel watched as the eight soldiers hastened their musket-loading in response to Charity's screaming. Their eyes were shifty and they whispered to each other quietly, finding the condemned traitor's cries eerily inappropriate.

"Anna! Dig into the ground with your toes like us!"

"Why?"

"Just do it!"

The soldiers finished loading their muskets and their captain called out to them in a hoarse yell. "Ready!"

Anna dug her toes into the dirt and her big toe pressed against the trigger of Charity's musket. She realized what her sister had done. She looked at James, whose head hung low as he was tied to the post.

"James! Wake up!"

"Aim!" the British captain yelled.

Just as the soldiers were about to shoot the four traitors, one of the soldiers aiming his rifle at them was hit in the chest by a bullet.

"Captain John Parker!" Charity exclaimed.

Captain Parker had rallied several local Minutemen to come to the rescue of the Johnstons and the other militiamen who were scheduled for execution this morning.

The British turned their line to face their oncoming enemy, but they could not see them at first. The Minutemen shot at them from concealed positions, behind bushes, trees, and buildings. Other British rushed from the barracks to try to flank their attackers.

The sound of gunfire so close roused James from his unconsciousness. "James!" Anna screamed. "Dig your toes into the dirt like me!"

"What?" He was cross-eyed with dizziness from the loss of blood.

One of the British soldiers, seeing no target from the field where shots were aimed at him, turned and pointed his musket at one of the four young traitors. He fired.

Blam!

"Anna!" Charity screamed.

Anna felt as if she had been hit by a car and struck by lightning at the same time. Her body was jarred from the force of the 50-caliber pellet that penetrated her body and sunk into the wood post. She gasped, and looked down at her life's blood spilling out of a hole in her upper stomach. She lost the feeling in her legs, and began to droop, being held up only by the wrist-ties that were hung up on a nail in the rear of the wood post. The pain turned to numbness, and her eyes closed. "Oh Jesus. Oh Jesus."

James was still barely conscious, unaware of what had happened to Anna. He appeared completely oblivious to his surroundings as bullets whizzed all around them. He turned his gaze toward Daniel and Charity, and his eyes appeared to be glossed over.

"James!" Daniel raised his voice with urgency. "Dig your toes into the dirt! Now! Do it!"

James shook his head and looked around. He saw several soldiers exchanging fire with militia in the distance. One of the red-coats was leveling his musket at Charity.

"Dig your toes into the dirt!"

James did as his siblings pleaded, and cut his toe on the edge of the bayonet of Charity's musket.

"Ow."

Suddenly, the dirt from the ground all around them was sucked up into the air as if by a tornado and began to spin violently. Their hands were freed of their bonds and the posts to which they were tied began to twist around them like a pretzel, and then spin around them at an increasing speed. The pain and dizziness in James' head was suddenly gone. Anna grabbed her stomach, and a smile came upon her face when she realized that she was perfectly fine.

"Ha ha ha!" James laughed as a sudden energy burst into his body. "You hid the gun in the dirt under our feet!"

Charity giggled with glee. "I love it when a plan comes together."

"Thank you Jesus!" Anna raised her hands triumphantly in the air. "I think I saw an angel. I was almost in heaven."

Charity and Anna pulled their younger brothers close as the whirlwind picked up speed and the noise grew loud.

Daniel, who was normally filled with fear at this phenomenon, seemed calm and relaxed. "Do you think we're headed home?"

Charity, overcome with gratitude for escaping death in the nick of time, wrapped her arms around Daniel and pulled him close. "I don't know."

When the dust began to slow, and the roar of the whirlwind began to settle around them, the sky was bright blue, and the heat of their new environment dropped down around them like a blanket of sweat. Boston's summer humidity was nothing compared to this. A long grassy field was on one side of them and on the other, a small town.

The sand from the whirlwind formed a ring around them on the ground, a yellow circle that completely surrounded them in a field of knee-high green grass. Interspersed haphazardly in the ring were splinters of wood from the wooden posts.

Suddenly, the loud bangs of rifles and pistols sounded on both sides of them.

"Not again." Charity gasped and pulled her siblings toward the ground. "Down! Everybody down!"

James crouched on the ground next to Anna. "Talk about out of the frying pan and into the fire."

That thought made Anna recall the bravery of Shadrach, Meshach, and Abednego in Nebuchadnezzar's fiery furnace, and she prayed quietly for strength and deliverance.

"I'm gonna find me some earmuffs!" James cupped his hands over his ears to shelter them from the loud gunshots all around. "This is crazy! At least we got our shoes back on now. Oh, look." He pointed to the musket Charity held in her hands.

"Keep your head down!" Charity ordered them.

"It's the same musket we found in our woods."

Charity looked at it and saw that it was indeed the same rifle that they had dug up from the bottom of their creek in Zanesville. She looked at the butt of the rifle and saw, however, that there was no engraving there. "We gotta find this 'Johnny' and get him to sign this thing for us so that we can go home."

"Where are we now?" James screamed to be heard over the bullets that whizzed non-stop over their heads and the cannon shells that exploded all around them.

Charity raised her head a little and looked in all directions briefly, and then ducked back down for the cover of the grass. "I don't know! I can barely see the soldiers through the high grass."

Anna placed a tight grip on Charity's forearm. "Daniel!" Charity saw that Anna's face was contorted with fear. Anna rose to her knees and looked quickly in all directions. "Where's Daniel?"

The children frantically searched around them in the grass for their little brother. "Daniel! Daniel!"

Daniel was missing.

Chapter 6

"Daniel's not here." Charity ducked low beneath the barrage of speeding bullets, and fixed her gaze upon an ant on the ground, bewildered, lost in wonder. She felt as small and insignificant in the grand scheme of history as that little ant was to this battle that they somehow dropped into. Why was God transporting them from battle to battle? What was God trying to teach them? And where was Daniel?

There was a momentary pause in the shooting. All Charity heard was the sound of her quickened pulse in her temples. Then she flinched at the unmistakable call coming from the direction of the field: "Charge!"

When the loud blasts of gunfire were replaced by the sound of running feet and the neighing of horses, Charity slowly stood. Toward the city she saw a line of cavalry wearing blue uniforms, and in the long green field she saw soldiers charging toward her, dressed in gray or brown tattered outfits. She pointed toward a line of trees away from the battle. "Run!"

The Johnstons began to sprint toward the tree line about a hundred yards away.

They had hardly run ten seconds when Charity screamed and fell to the ground. "Ow! Oh no."

Anna stopped and bent down to check on her sister. "What happened?"

"I couldn't see that hole in the high grass." She motioned toward a groundhog hole behind her. "I think I broke my ankle."

"Come on." James and Anna tried to help her up.

141

"No." Charity pushed him away, and then grabbed her swelling ankle. "It hurts too bad. You run! Go!"

"No," Anna protested. "We are not leaving you, Charity." Bullets began to whiz past them again, causing them to duck lower into the grass.

"They're coming." James could just see the heads of the soldiers charging toward them over the field.

Charity was resolved as she clutched her ankle. "I guess it's my turn to get captured, Anna. Now, take the musket to keep it safe, and go! Protect your brother! Find Daniel! Don't worry, God'll bring us together again."

Anna and James resumed their sprint toward the tree line, just escaping the collision of Union and Confederate soldiers.

* * * * *

Anna and James watched the battle from the cover of the trees, hoping for someone to retreat so they could rescue Charity, but the conflict was bitter and enduring. Men shot each other, sliced each other with swords, and survivors of the hailstorm of bullets grappled with each other on the ground. It was bloody and gruesome. There were many fatalities on both sides, and the moans and cries of the wounded filled the air, bringing tears of grief to the eyes of the two Johnston children.

Anna squinted through her wet eyes and searched the field for any sign of Charity amidst the clutter, the scattered weapons, and the corpses of the dead and dying men and horses. "Charity's out there." Large tears swam their way down Anna's cheeks. "We've got to save her."

"We will." James patted her on the shoulder. "But we need to use wisdom."

The Confederates sent reinforcements into the battle and completely drove back the Union cavalry with superior numbers.

The Union forces were pushed back through the town of Gettysburg and regrouped south of the town along the high ground beside a cemetery. They dug in as Confederates took stock of their wounded and strengthened their positions. Generals and officers gathered and conspired on the eve of the most famous battle of the American Civil War.

When the Confederates pressed forward toward Gettysburg, James patted Anna on the arm. "Now's our chance, sister. Let's go find–"

"Halt!" The cry from behind chilled them to the bone. "Get to your feet. Slowly. And put that gun on the ground!" Anna and James heard the clicking sound of pistols being cocked behind them.

Anna pushed the musket away from her, and the two Johnstons held their breath as they stood and turned with their hands in the air. A Union officer on horseback kept his finger firm against the trigger of his pistol as he aimed it at the taller of the two children. He had sharp brown eyes under a furry brow, and his beard was trimmed and waxed so perfectly it almost looked artificial.

"Martin!" The officer called out to a subordinate twenty yards behind them on foot. "Arrest them. They're Confederate spies. Take them into Gettysburg and commandeer the prison to hold them."

"Yes sir."

"We're not spies," Anna exclaimed. "We don't even know where we are."

"More evidence of your guilt! Everyone within twenty miles knows what's stirring up around here with the Confederate Army's march to Washington."

"Patience." An older gray-haired officer walked his horse up beside the other officer. "Let them tell us what they are doing here."

James stuttered an incoherent response, glancing uneasily at his equally speechless sister. They were unprepared for the question, and didn't know how to best answer it. The truth seemed to be the most absurd of all things to say. They'd wind up in an insane asylum if they told them the truth. In the officers' minds, their reluctance to forthrightly answer the question confirmed their guilt.

The elderly officer was growing impatient. "Speak!"

Anna finally gave a non-answer. "We're from Ohio."

"From Ohio? Where? Southern Ohio?"

Anna nodded. "I was born in Portsmouth, the southern-most city."

"Southern Ohio is full of copperhead traitors. You're under arrest. Take them away."

"This is crazy!" James exclaimed. "This is supposed to be the land of the free and home of the brave. This is supposed to be the country of the people, by the people, and for the people. We did not do anything wrong!"

"Take them away."

A journalist who worked as a part-time speechwriter for President Lincoln rode on horseback just behind the officers. He was mesmerized at the words of the orange-headed boy, and he jotted down the words. These words would turn out to be the most memorable words of Lincoln's speech to be given soon after the conclusion of this battle.

Anna stared at the young man who took her special musket. The lad laid the mysterious musket on the ground as he tied their hands behind their backs. As they were led toward town, Anna longingly eyed the special musket that the young man carried over his shoulder. If they lost that musket, they'd never be able to get home.

Anna thought it wise to try and make friends with the young lad. "That musket you are holding, sir, is very special to me. I hope I can get it back when we are cleared of wrong-doing."

The young man winked at her and whispered, "You didn't do anything wrong. I believe you. The officers are just paranoid. They know that a big battle's brewing, and they might not win it."

* * * * *

"What in the world are you doing out here in a field of battle, young lady?"

Charity looked up at the 14-year-old Kentucky militiaman, whose scruffy goatee and unwashed face made him look more like a starving homeless beggar than a soldier of war. After pushing back the Union cavalry, the Confederates were taking stock of the dead and wounded when this scrawny Kentuckian found Charity in the middle of the field, holding her ankle with one hand and with the other, clutching the hand of a wounded Confederate soldier to comfort him.

"Help this fellow first."

"Hey, Thomas." The Kentuckian called out to a friend who was nearby. "Got someone over here who needs your help." He motioned toward the injured Confederate soldier. The Kentucky soldier then turned his attention to the thin redheaded girl who lay on the ground before him. In the midst of all this masculine blue and gray, blood and guts, sweat and stink, her fair complexion and flowing reddish hair was quite a sight to behold. She mesmerized him. Charity felt uncomfortable as he stared at her, a faint grin upon his thin face. He finally bent down to check her ankle.

"I've got to find my family. Can you loan me a horse? They headed toward that tree line over there when your forces charged." She pointed to the tree line with an outstretched hand.

"Only our officers have horses, ma'am," he said as he palpated her ankle. "Besides, that area is under Union control right now."

Union control? Charity winced as the young man checked her swollen ankle for evidence of a fracture.

"Your ankle doesn't feel broken. It's just sprained. It'll swell for sure. You ain't seen the worst of that."

The Kentuckian assisted her to her feet and helped her walk back toward where the Confederates were regrouping, waiting for reinforcements. "Where are we?"

"Pennsylvania, ma'am. I'm sorry you got messed up in the crossfire. We were headed to Gettysburg for shoes, but then we ran into their cavalry. We're blind to their numbers, but we swept what we could see of them off the field, didn't we?"

"Is that Gettysburg?" She pointed to the small town across the field.

He looked at her cock-eyed for a moment, surprised that she didn't know the answer to that question. "Yes it is, ma'am. Where are you from anyway?"

Charity suddenly realized that she was on the verge of the major battle that turned the course of the Civil War and forced a reluctant President Lincoln to end slavery in the south.

"This battle will turn the tide of the war against you, and you're going to lose it if you march to Gettysburg to face the federal army."

The young soldier stopped and looked the redhead in the eye. "How do *you* know *that*?"

"I know all about the Civil War."

"The Civil War? Ha!" the Kentuckian laughed mockingly. "This war ain't the least bit civil. This is the War of Northern Aggression. All we ever wanted was to be left alone. They" – he pointed toward the hills where the feds were digging their fortifications – "invaded our state as if it belonged to them."

"The victors will write the history books, sir, your invader will practically be elevated to sainthood. If you march to Gettysburg, the history books will be the least of your worries."

The soldier looked at her like she was crazy, and Charity realized that she had a rare opportunity for a firsthand look at the facts from the losing side. Then she began to wonder if she could actually turn the tide of the war with her counsel. After all, if she could persuade the Confederates to turn back from Gettysburg and get back to a defensive position, they may just hold out to win it. She tried to imagine a United States of America where the federal government was the servant of the states as the forefathers intended, instead of the states being controlled by a massive central government. But then her mind wandered to the plight of the American slave. How much longer would it take for them to be freed if it weren't for Lincoln's Emancipation Proclamation?

"Where are you from, young lady?"

"Ohio."

"Ohio? They're in the Union." The Kentuckian wondered for a moment whether Charity was a spy.

"My Dad's from South Carolina and Mom's from Georgia. I'm sympathetic."

"You a copperhead?" A copperhead was a term that referred to northerners who were sympathetic with the south.

"I suppose."

"Was your Dad at Ft. Sumter?" Ft. Sumter was where the first shot of the Civil War was fired.

Charity chuckled at the thought of her Dad in field cams at Ft. Sumter with his AR-15 and ten thirty-round clips. "With my Dad's semi-automatic, and with his kids re-loading for him, he could have taken out every soldier on this battle field today."

The young Kentuckian had a confused look on his fuzzy face. "Semi-what?"

"It's a musket that fires without reloading. Bang-bang-bang-bang-bang! It shoots real fast."

"I've never heard of such a thing. Do you have this weapon?"

Charity grinned at the young man's enthusiasm. "You need to take me to General Lee. I can help you more than you know."

As Charity limped into the area where the injured were being treated, she saw a slave carrying water for the Confederate physician. She stopped, and stared in shock at the idea of this little black boy being treated like an animal, carrying a bucket of water from a nearby stream.

The thin boy stumbled on a soldier's bag of musket balls and spilled his bucket of water. He growled in disgust with himself. "So sorry! So sorry!"

Charity bent down to help him up, and when the black boy laid eyes on her, he exclaimed, "Sister!" He threw his arms around her neck. Charity was aghast. "It's me, Daniel!"

She pulled him back and looked into his black eyes. "Daniel? What happened to you? You're a black boy!"

Before Daniel could answer, the physician, whose water bucket Daniel spilled, stomped over and gave Daniel a kick in the side of his leg. Daniel fell to the ground and cowered beside a table where a wounded soldier lay, raising his hands to try and block any blows that his furious master may rain upon him.

"You foolish pest! I told you to be careful!" The physician grabbed a rifle off the ground and prepared to swing the butt of it at the little black boy.

"Stop that!" Charity hollered at the physician. The physician took one look at the redheaded girl, and then continued his thrashing of the black boy, who was skin and bones.

He smacked the stock of the gun against the poor boy's arms and legs as the boy continued to cry out. "So sorry! So sorry!"

"Help him! He's my, he's my..." Charity pulled on the sleeve of the young Kentuckian beside her as she tried to limp to the little black boy's aid. "You wouldn't just sit by while he beat his dog like that, would you?"

"He's not our property. It's not our problem."

"Property?" Charity was disgusted at the idea that one human being could be another human being's property. "He's my brother!"

The Kentuckian looked at Charity as if she had just pronounced the earth flat. "Your brother?"

The injured soldier on the table leaned toward Charity, and said, "You're not one of them fanatical abolitionists, are ya?"

The physician stopped beating the black boy, and the poor slave whimpered softly, caressing his lacerations. "Now, let's try it again. Fetch me a bucket of water and exercise more caution this time."

"Yes sir!" The black slave resumed his duties with very little self-pity. He picked up his water bucket and limped along toward the creek.

The physician made his way toward Charity as he wiped the sweat off his brow. "Well, what happened to your ankle, girl?"

"I wouldn't accept help from you if you were the last doctor on earth, you pathetic beast!" Charity's eyes welled up with tears as she reproved the slave-owner more harshly than she would have if her emotions were under better control. "That boy slipped on accident. You were so cruel to him. How would you like it if you were treated that way?"

The physician puffed out his cheeks and turned in disgust from the nosy little redheaded girl.

Charity's gaze darted to the Kentuckian, who appeared amazed at the girl's brazen courage. "Do you agree?"

The Kentuckian looked down at the ground, appearing either too bashful or too fearful to take her side in the discussion. He leaned close to her and whispered, "You are going to get yourself in some trouble, young lady, if you go upbraiding grown men like that around here!"

Her nose hairs burned at the young Confederate's pungent breath. "Please take me to General Lee. I have information that can help them win this battle."

"Let's get your ankle bound and get you a crutch first. I think the General would like to hear about this repeating weapon your father has."

"Just get me a crutch. I'm not letting this miserable monster salve his conscience by bandaging my busted ankle." Charity hobbled over to a stack of crutches outside of a nearby tent. She bent down and picked one up, almost falling over in the process. She tucked the crutch under one of her arms, and said, "Take me to General Lee."

* * * * *

When Charity first laid her eyes on him in the midst of his generals and captains, debating the best plan of attack, she was initially awed. But when General Robert E. Lee prevailed in his plan to advance against the Union forces, she could be silent no longer.

"General Lee!" she interrupted him. All eyes turned to her. "I'm sorry to interrupt, but I must warn you. You will lose this war if you attack them at Gettysburg."

A general stepped between Lee and the girl. "Who is this child that speaks uninvited in the presence of Confederate generals?"

Charity stepped forward with the help of her hand-made crutch to introduce herself more formally, but the Kentuckian who rescued her spoke first. "We found her injured in the field of this morning's skirmish, General Lee." He appeared embarrassed that Charity had dared to interrupt General Lee in the midst of communicating his plan of attack to the Confederate army leaders.

"I know how this battle will transpire and you will not be able to break the Union position on Cemetery Ridge, nor on their flanks." She leaned uneasily on her hand-made crutch. "They have the high ground, General Lee."

All eyes were fastened on Charity in awe. An awkward moment passed when Charity glanced at the general by the door, and said, "I read it in a book."

"A book?"

"Yeah." Charity took a deep breath and mumbled, "I also saw the movie."

"We could be one battle away from independence," the gray-bearded General Lee said with a confident smirk. The word "independence" gave Charity a déjà vu sensation. That's the same terminology the colonists used to describe their conflict with the British. But this war was best known for freeing the slaves. She reminded herself that to the South, this conflict was about independence from federal authority. "We could be one skirmish away from the end of this war, and you try to frighten us into retreat without any evidence? We don't even know their strengths."

"So you're going to flip a coin with the lives of your men? Shouldn't you discover their numbers *before* you devise a plan to attack? Retreat, find better ground, and save your men."

General Lee became frustrated that a mysterious redheaded girl that no one knew had the audacity to sabotage his plan to attack before he could even explain it to the gathering of Confederate leaders. "We will probably out-number the Union troops. General Picket will be here soon with 15,000 fresh troops if the conflict even lasts till he arrives."

"General Pickets' troops will be slaughtered when you charge Cemetery Ridge."

"When?" General Lee's breathing rate quickened.

Charity blushed, and then corrected herself. "If."

"That's absurd." General Lee sliced a hand through the humid air. The other generals and captains nodded in view of their leader's confidence.

"You think you are invincible because of the previous battles you have won, but they were defensive conflicts, General. You have not learned the lesson of General Benedict Arnold in the Revolutionary War. He was victorious in his defensive campaigns, but when he led an offensive campaign into Canada to take Quebec, his men were wasted. When you, General Lee, were defensive you won, but when the Confederacy went on the offense, you lost. Remember Antietam, in Maryland? Here you have ascended into Union territory again."

General Lee appeared insulted that the girl would refer to the Confederates as the invaders. *"They* are the invaders, ma'am!" He punched his index finger northeast with each indictment of the federal government. "It was Lincoln who violated the Constitution when he called up troops without congressional authorization. It was Lincoln who levied money for war and called for a blockade without congressional authorization, contrary to the Constitution. This Abraham Lincoln makes King George the Third look like a friend of democracy by contrast! Every argument that justified our secession from Great Britain justifies the south's secession today."

"With all due respect, General Lee, you protest the North's tyranny, but how many African-Americans have been kidnapped by Muslim gangs on the coast of Africa, and sold to ships bound for your states?"

African-Americans? These Confederate generals had never heard black slaves referred to in such a way, and by the way they shifted and murmured, Charity could tell they didn't like it one bit.

"How many of them have been murdered, or had the skin

ripped off their backs by your slave masters' whips - all with the Confederacy's blessing?"

General Lee pointed his index finger in Charity's face, and the other generals took a step backward as they saw him more enraged than they had ever seen him before. "I'm against slavery! I've always been against it, and I've spoken against it. This conflict is *not* about slavery! I was offered the leadership position of the Union's army before they invaded Virginia. Everyone knows I'm against secession. I'm here in defense of Virginia, not slavery, and not secession. It's the federal government's Dred Scott Supreme Court decision that called a black man 'property' and that is why the Underground Railroad has to go all the way to Canada to find free land for the Negroes." Some generals in the room shifted uneasily as General Lee spoke favorably of the Underground Railroad, which freed slaves contrary to Confederate law. "President Lincoln has personally supported a constitutional amendment to perpetuate slavery in the states where it is practiced. No slave was ever sold or bought under a Confederate flag. The Confederate constitution bans the import of slaves. The federal Constitution does not..."

"Mark my words, General Lee. A little leaven will leaven the whole lump. Achan's sin caused all Israel to flee before the men of Ai. The Confederate Army will lose this war unless the Confederacy repents of the sin of slavery and you embrace your black brothers and sisters in Christian love." With those words, faces flushed and men grunted and murmured uneasily. "You cannot appeal to the unjust tyranny of the north as a justification for rebelling if you have the mote in your own eye, for as you judge, you will be judged. God will never bless hypocrisy."

Another general stepped forward, frustrated that this radical little abolitionist was setting the agenda of their officer's meeting. "This sin is on both sides of the Mason Dixon."

"And that justifies the Confederacy's evil?"

"No, it does not." General Lee appeared introspective as he massaged his gray beard. He felt his legs go rubbery and his heart sped up. He looked up at Charity and her eyes were fixed upon him. It appeared that this girl's eyes were as sharp as her words, piercing flesh and exposing the sin in the deepest part of his heart.

"The Confederacy and the Union both have the blood of the

innocent on their hands," Charity remarked. "If the Confederates do not repent of the sin of slavery, you will lose tens of thousands of fathers and sons and you will lose this battle and this war. God will deliver the slaves anyway. When this conflict ends, President Lincoln will announce the Emancipation Proclamation, freeing the slaves and—"

"He wouldn't dare!" The Confederate generals found that unbelievable.

"He will, and in it he will free every slave in every southern state who does not return to the Union. And he will win the sympathy of France and England, whom you know will not support the Confederacy because of your slavery." Charity paused to observe the coldness of their countenances. They had hardened their heart to the truth. "Please." She made a fist with both hands and pleaded with them. "You must end slavery or you will lose this war!"

A messenger suddenly burst into the room with an urgent message for General Lee. "General Longstreet sends word! He has engaged at Peach Orchard and is pushing back the Union forces!"

A cheer erupted throughout the room at the news. Only Charity and General Lee were silent.

"His men are engaged at Little Round Top. Intense action is afoot at Wheat Field and Devil's Den."

General Lee turned to the map on the wall to mark out the positions as the generals gathered near, preparing for orders.

"But General Lee!" Charity raised her voice to try to get their attention again.

"I'm sorry, little missy." Lee stepped closer to her and smiled at her more warmly than the other generals expected him to. "Would to God that He had such a voice when we formed the Confederacy. But I am not a monarch and cannot make unilateral decisions, especially on the eve of today's conflict. We must turn our attention to the day's demands. You're a prophetess out of season. Perhaps we shall discuss more of this matter later." General Lee turned to the young Kentuckian who accompanied her. "Take her out of here."

"Yes, General Lee."

The Kentuckian wrapped his lanky fingers around her bicep and directed her from the tent. "Let's go, prophetess-out-of-season."

Charity looked up at him and wondered if he was praising or mocking her.

* * * * *

Anna and James spent the night in prison with many copper-heads. A well-dressed local informed Anna that he was the mayor of a nearby town and had been arrested simply for opposing the invasion of the south.

"What?" Anna couldn't believe that a democratically elected mayor could be put in jail for simply verbally opposing the war.

"I wanted the south to stay in the Union - I did! But I was against invading the south to keep it unified. The southern states entered the Union voluntarily, and they have the right to leave voluntarily and govern themselves. That was Thomas Jefferson's position a hundred years ago. The states are the masters of the federal government, not the other way around."

"What about Ft. Sumter?" James asked. "Wasn't it the south who fired first?"

"No one was even killed at Ft. Sumter." The mayor looked James in the eye. "Tell me, if someone comes into your home uninvited brandishing a weapon, don't you have a right to defend yourself?" James nodded. "The south had already seceded peacefully, but northern troops insisted on occupying Ft. Sumter so they could levy taxes on ships coming into the bay. The south had every right to resist."

"That seems like common sense to me," said Anna.

"Well, President Lincoln considers that opinion to be treason. They won't even let me see a lawyer or give me a trial date."

"What about free speech?" James asked.

"Free speech, hah!" The mayor puffed out his cheeks and exhaled noisily. "Lincoln has shut down newspapers and arrested over ten thousand northerners and held them without charge, without bail, and without a trial by jury, simply because they were against the war. He had the audacity to arrest many Maryland legislators on the eve of their vote to join the south. That's one way to make sure the vote goes in your favor – arrest everyone who's going to vote against you! When judges in Maryland began to look into the circumstances surrounding the crooked elections, Lincoln ordered the judges to be arrested too. You're from Ohio, right?"

"Yes sir."

"Lincoln arrested the democratic candidate for governor in Ohio, a Mr., uh," – he snapped his fingers and tried to recall the name – "Vallandigham, that's it. What was his crime? He spoke out against Lincoln's invasion. Lincoln even signed an arrest warrant against Chief Justice Taney of the Supreme Court for deciding that Lincoln's suspension of a right to a trial by jury was unlawful. If that's not the color of tyranny, then I'm colorblind. Our democratic republic no longer exists. We are under a dictatorship now."

* * * * *

Charity's ankle started feeling better, and she began to roam around the outdoor hospital area with the help of her crutch, trying to comfort soldiers who continued to be brought back from the front lines of the conflict. It was there that she finally saw the slave boy again. He was carrying a bucket of water in both hands.

"Daniel!"

He saw her and said, "Shhh. I'll get beat wit' a stick if you talk to me."

"What happened to you? How did you–"

"I don't know," he whispered to her, struggling under the weight of the heavy buckets. "Woke up this way."

"Well, may I help you with that?" She reached to take one of the buckets of water out of his hands before he had a chance to respond.

"Ah. Thank you." He did not make eye contact with her and was careful not to be too appreciative, as his master forbade him to fraternize with whites. He glanced at her and gave her a quick smile and then looked back down at his bucket as tears welled up in his eyes. "Oh Charity, my people are suffering so much."

"*Your* people?"

"Ma mudder's sick, and they won't take care of her. They'll beat her if she slows. My little brothers and sisters aren't given clothes until they're big enough to work. They don't teach readin' or writin'. They treat us like animals, no warmth at all."

"Where's your family?"

"Ma mudder's one of the cooks." He motioned toward the rear of the camp. "They keeled ma fadda on da boat."

Charity's heart dropped when she considered how much grief these people must have had to endure. "Daniel, you're even starting to sound like a slave. You're not a slave though. You're my brother."

Daniel looked offended. Tears welled up in his bloodshot eyes. "The slaves are your brothers and sisters too. They love God. Help us."

They set down their buckets in the physician's tent, and she knelt down beside him so she could look up into his eyes. She smiled warmly at him. "I'm so sorry, Daniel."

He grinned sheepishly, and his two front white teeth lit up his brown face like a car's headlights coming down the road at night. "I miss you."

The physician saw Charity speaking to his slave and he bolted over toward them. Charity saw him coming and stood between them. "I want Daniel."

"Who?"

She pointed at the frail black slave.

"His name's Eli. What do you mean you want Eli?" The physician was stunned.

Daniel was equally surprised. He put his head down and looked at the ground, careful not to incite his master's wrath again. Many soldiers who were recuperating from wounds nearby listened intently to the redhead's offer.

"I thought you were against buying slaves, little girl."

"I'm not against buying their freedom."

That comment broke a floodwall of thigh-slapping laughs and jeers that made Charity's face turn red. The physician could hardly contain himself.

"I'm serious!"

"Well, can you afford him, little missie?"

Charity reached into her pocket for her MP3 player, hoping to amaze the doctor with the technology as she had amazed King Saul, but her MP3 player was missing. She must have lost it on the battlefield. "I, I, uh, I don't have any money, but I'll take his place. I'm older and more experienced. I can shoot and cook."

"What?" Daniel couldn't believe his ears. "You take ma place?"

"Take his place?" The physician was equally perplexed.

"Yes. I'll work for you till I'm eighteen."

"But he's mine for life!"

"All right, then, I'll work for you for life, at least until my brothers and sisters can buy my freedom."

"You are white. Would your parents approve of your foolish offer?"

"My parents would praise me for my Christ-like love."

"You have a limp from your sprained ankle. How can you fetch water as quickly as Eli?"

"I can try."

"How are you going to take care of him when you're serving me? Where will he go? He's a slave. His mother's a slave. He's a black boy in a white man's world. He's uneducated."

"He's a human being made in God's image!" She screamed it out, slapping her thighs for emphasis. "Where's your pity? He needs love. He needs a Dad, not an owner."

"He's a Negro!" the physician spat while pointing at the skinny black boy. "Darwin proved that blacks are inferior to whites."

"Eli's got a human mind, a human heart, human blood, and human hands and feet. He's capable of believing the Gospel of Jesus Christ. He's capable of love and justice."

"He's a Negro!"

Charity's mouth went dry as she saw the doctor's face blush with frustration at having to explain to her what was so obvious to him. "Only a fool rejects the Bible for atheistic theories like evolution. God made man in His own image and we are all of Adam's race." She placed a hand on the young black boy's shoulder. "That's what the Bible says."

"Folly! Superstitious folly!" The physician returned to the side of a groaning patient.

"And your blasphemy against God's Word isn't?"

The physician snapped back without looking at her: "Both of you fetch me some more water or I'll give Eli a beating on your behalf."

"Yes, Massa." The boy bowed low and picked up two empty buckets, and then turned and rushed down the trail that led to the creek.

The physician sneered at the redheaded girl and she bowed to him. "I wouldn't want to be in your shoes on Judgment Day for all the wealth and fame in the world." She reached down, picked up two empty buckets, and tried to catch up to little Eli, her sore ankle paining her as she limped.

Her mind began to buzz as she began to scheme an escape plan for Eli and his family.

* * * * *

At the crack of dawn, the boy who had tied the hands of Anna and James snuck into the prison through an open window in the foyer to check on them.

"Hey, Martin." Anna waved at him cheerfully.

"Shhh. I'm not allowed to be here." He glanced over his shoulder, worried that the soldier guarding outside the front door would hear the noise, come in, and investigate.

"We aren't spies." James reached through the bars to shake his hand. "You gotta free us."

He handed the two Johnstons a piece of bread. "I came to see how you're doing."

Anna split the piece of bread and gave the larger of the two halves to James. "Where's the musket you took from me, Martin?"

"Oh. I wanted to keep it for myself so I could safeguard it, but an officer saw me with it and put it in the stockpile of other muskets."

Anna and James looked at each other fearfully. "We've got to get that gun, Martin."

"I tried to get them to think it was mine, but they took it. My dad, who died in the last battle, told the captain before he passed that he preferred that I serve through helping with the injured rather than shooting in combat. At least until the captain thinks I'm ready to fight."

"Oh. I'm sorry about your dad."

"Shhh. I've got to go."

"Wait," said James. "You've got to break us out of here."

"If I tried that, I'd be in that cell next to you, or shot dead as a traitor." The young man turned to hop out of the open window.

"Please, we need that gun and we need to get out of here." Anna begged to no avail as Martin quickly exited.

Just as he disappeared through the window, a soldier barged into the room. He glanced into each of the cells, and then ordered them: "Be quiet!"

* * * * *

"Let me help you escape." Charity pleaded with the slave boy's mother as the sun began to set on the Confederate soldiers' camp. "I can help you."

"No way! They bees killin us if we do dat."

Charity ducked into the slave family's tattered tent to try to persuade the mother to let her help her and her four children escape from bondage. The children were lying on the floor around them on bundles of musty hay. They looked up at Charity wide-eyed, having never before seen a white child enter their lodging. "You can pretend like you're my slaves until we make it to Canada."

"Tay have slave laws. Da government will arrest you for having us wit you when you don't own us."

"Please," Charity said, now begging. "Let me help you be free."

The middle-aged black woman, dressed in tattered rags, grabbed Charity's shoulders and smiled. "You are a lovin girl, but we live for heaven, missy. We are free inside, in here." The thin woman patted her chest. "We donts live for this ol' world. We are more blessed dan you. You have many riches and friends and tings. We only have Jesus – dats it! We are alright with Jesus."

"But your children—"

"If ma babies live for Jesus, tay be alright too. If you wanna help us, then when you bring up your own babes, teach dem love."

A tear came to Charity's eye, and she pulled the black woman close and gave her a hug, while her children gazed at them in awe. She saw tears welling up in Daniel's eyes, and tried to imagine what life would be like for him if he were never freed. "I shall pray for you to be free, all of you." She pulled away and looked into her eyes. "I'm so glad to know you, my sister." Charity tried in vain to hold back the sob that swelled in her throat.

Daniel walked to Charity and hugged her from behind with all his might. Charity patted his head. "I love you, little brother. You trust in Jesus and obey your Momma. Freedom will come for you if you trust in God." She leaned close and whispered in his ear. "I'll find a way to get you soon. You've got to be there when we find the musket."

He pulled away from her and looked into her eyes. "But how?"

"Don't worry. Trust God."

The black woman had never seen a white person exhibit such affection for them before. She raised her hands to heaven and laughed. "Praise da Lord! Ah, ma girl! You are so special to da Lord and to me."

Charity returned the smile, then drew near to her and whispered in her ear. "Listen. Tomorrow morning's battle will give the Confederates a great loss. When they lose, the slaves will be freed in the Confederate states."

"What? How do you know dis?"

"Your day of jubilee is closer than you think, sister. Tell all your fellow slaves to pray. The Emancipation Proclamation is coming. Freedom is coming to your people."

The woman's mouth gaped open and she gazed into Charity's eyes to try to discern whether she was being sincere. "We will pray so."

"Try to see to it that Eli's on the front lines, helping with the injured. Can you do that?"

The black woman frowned and shook her head. "Dats not up to me, sister. Das up to the Massa."

* * * * *

At the break of dawn on the third day, the cannons began to shake the very ground all around Gettysburg.

"It has begun." Anna put her arms over her brother as they huddled together on the ground. "Let's stay away from the walls and stay low."

"How is Charity going to find us?"

"I don't know. Let's pray."

* * * * *

Charity was so upset when she discovered that General Lee spurned her warnings and was sending Pickett's fifteen thousand men right up the middle of the Union's lines to try to break them at Cemetery Ridge. Five thousand Union soldiers huddled on that ridge, and the Confederates would be under heavy cannon fire and musket fire for much of the long distance across the field. The feds would have the cover of a stone wall with the ability to take careful aim while lying down. The Confederates, on the other hand, would be shooting while dodging cannon shrapnel on a wide-open field. She knew this would be a decision that General Lee would regret, but there was nothing she could do about it now. Her only concern now was finding her brothers and her sister and that musket so they could go home.

But how would she meet up with her siblings in the midst of all of the killing? How would she ever be able to find them across the battle line? Where was the musket? This was like trying to put a puzzle together with only half of the pieces. Her only move was to pray and trust in the Lord. She must believe that the Lord was going to drop one piece of the puzzle in her lap at a time.

She decided that she *had* to join the Confederates on the charge up the middle. She knew as a historical fact that many of the Confederates did make it to the clump of trees on Cemetery Ridge. If she could be among them, maybe she could feign an injury, avoid detection, and sneak her way around their lines through the smoke and fury to find her brother and sister in the Union's camp. But how was she going to get back to Daniel?

After changing into a Confederate uniform and putting her red hair up in a bun, she huddled behind some bushes with her friend from Kentucky. She saw General Pickett, bellowing cheers and rallying his men into a frenzy, and she pitied them. *If only their leaders would defend 'the least of these', maybe God would defend them.*

The cannon fire from the Union slowed, and the Confederate generals prayed that they had taken out their cannons on their front lines. That was exactly what the Union forces wanted them to think. In reality, the north was just conserving ammunition.

The trumpet sounded and General Pickett issued the order to begin marching toward the enemy. They stepped out on the grassy field and began to make their way across the long, flat, open field.

Charity stayed low to the ground, knowing what was to come. She was not given a weapon, but was told that if she wanted to join the march to Cemetery Ridge, she would find a weapon lying on the ground soon enough. She consented, realizing that not having a weapon might actually increase her chances for survival.

* * * * *

A Confederate cannonball came speeding through the roof and landed right in the foyer of the small prison where Anna and James huddled, sending shrapnel in every direction and knocking the front of their jail cell door off its hinges. Men in nearby cells began to scream in terror. The prisoners were deafened by the blast for a moment, but none of them were injured.

James came to his senses and realized that the guard who watched them in the office area had been killed by the blast.

"It's time to go now." James grabbed his sister by the shoulders. "God has split the Red Sea for us."

Anna was in shock. The huge blast scared her half to death. James helped her up and prodded her through the open cell door.

"Let me out too!" Others in nearby cells began to call out to James as he stepped out of his cell. He went to the Union guard who had been killed by cannon shrapnel, took the keys off of his belt, and began to unlock the other cell doors. Another cannonball landed just outside the prison, forcing them all to hug the ground again for fear of shrapnel.

"Come on!" James waved Anna toward the front door of the prison. "We gotta find that musket."James peeked out of the broken prison door, and saw men were running to and fro, seeking care for the injured, relaying orders, or rushing with their muskets to the front lines. "How are we gonna find Martin?"

Anna shook off her fear and took a deep breath. "We just can't go waltzing around a war zone, James."

The mayor opened a closet and found a stock of ammunition. "Just grab a bucket of musket balls. Walk around with these while you're looking for your friend. Maybe carry some gauze under your belt. They'll think you're helping the Union forces." The mayor ran to the front door and prepared to bolt for freedom. "Be careful, or you might get shot by the Confederates!"

* * * * *

The cannon from the Union forces on Cemetery Ridge soon began to create huge holes in the Confederate lines. The southerners picked up the pace across the field and filled the gaps, but when they got closer, the Union packed small iron balls into the cannon, making the weapon like a huge shotgun. Dozens of Confederate soldiers were cut to ribbons with each shot.

Charity tried to stay low to the ground. She saw thousands of Union soldiers hugging the ground ahead of her, carefully aiming their muskets at them as they charged. Her heart pounded with fear.

An officer became fed up with so many Confederates dying without even firing a shot, so he lined his men up and ordered a volley. The distance was too far for accuracy, and the Union soldiers made small targets as they stayed low to the stone wall. Then the Union soldiers responded with a unified volley and viciously cut through the Confederate forces. A Confederate charge was ordered and they ran into a torrent of speeding lead. A red mist filled the air from the collision of Union bullets and the flesh of the charging southerners.

Charity kept her sights on the clump of trees on the ridge. She ran low to the ground beside the Kentuckian. They followed on the heels of dozens of Confederate soldiers who vigorously wielded their bayonets against the Union soldiers. With the Union soldiers so close in combat and lack of time to reload, most of the shooting was left to the officers' pistols. The pace slowed with the vicious hand-to-hand combat, and they gradually drew near to the clump of trees.

Charity ducked a swing of a Union soldier's sword. The blade scraped her hat and knocked it off. "Hey! I'm a girl!"

"A girl!" The Union soldier's chest heaved with exertion. "What are you doing out—" A Confederate soldier distracted him with a swing of his bayonet and they ended up on the ground grappling with each other.

An officer with a pistol started firing into the Confederates and one of them was struck and landed on top of her. The shrieks of the warriors, the explosion of the bombs and bullets, and the bitter smell of burning gunpowder made her close her eyes, put her hands over her ears, and scream a prayer to God for mercy. She cried for the killing to end.

* * * * *

As James and Anna carried their buckets, gauze, and ammunition, toward the front lines looking for Martin, the sound of the gunfire, the shouts of the fighters, and the groans of the injured became unbearable. Anna finally saw Martin dragging an injured soldier away from the front lines.

"Martin!" She ran up to him.

"How'd you get free?"

"Don't worry about that. Where's my gun?"

"I don't know." He crouched low. "Keep your head down! The Confederates are charging."

"Here, we'll help you." Anna motioned for James to grab the injured soldier's legs and they dragged him away from the front lines toward a horse-drawn flatbed on which they were laying the wounded. "You gotta help me find that musket, Martin!"

"Why?"

"It's important!"

"The officer took all the muskets to the front line. I don't know where it is. Oh no! Look!" He pointed toward a clump of trees to their right. "The Confederates are breaking through!" They caught a glimpse of gray and brown-shirted southerners through the line of blue. The pistol fire began to pick up and Union officers rallied troops into a line behind the clump of trees in preparation for a charge. The cries of the soldiers in battle grew nearer.

"Come on!" James began to jog toward the action simply for the thrill of being close to danger. Martin reluctantly followed as he searched the ground for a dropped musket to shoot or a sword to wield.

"What are you doing? Get back here!" Anna cried out to James, but he did not slow. She followed him and ducked behind an ammo cart beside him. Her eyes brightened when she saw a familiar color in the throng of blue and gray. She pointed into the midst of the struggling warriors. "Charity! There's Charity!"

Through the legs of several fighting soldiers, they saw a patch of long, red hair, flowing in the easterly breeze. "Charity!" Charity was on her knees between two dead bodies, and had her face buried in her hands. James looked at Anna, his eyes wide with concern for their big sister. "I think she's hurt."

Without warning, James raced into the bloodbath, bounding over the corpses and around the dueling soldiers like a young buck avoiding cars while passing over a busy highway.

"James! What are you doing!?" Anna screamed at him. "You're going to get yourself killed!" Anna turned to Martin, who huddled close to the ground behind the barrel beside her. "Pray that God'll keep us safe." She then darted into the fray.

A Confederate wielding a musket at a Union soldier almost whacked James in the head. He ducked it at the last second and fell at Charity's side. "Charity!"

"Oh James!" She clutched him tightly.

Momentarily, Anna dropped on the ground beside them. "Let's get outta here!"

"No!" Charity grabbed Anna's arm. "Stay low until the conflict subsides!"

A Confederate soldier suddenly fell across Charity's legs, mortally wounded. He grasped a sword, and Anna thought that Charity had inadvertently been run through with it. Martin pulled the soldier off of her, and they discovered that she was all right. The ground was covered with the slain or those writhing in pain, and yet the hand-to-hand combat was still fierce all around them. Two lines of Union soldiers ten yards away prepared to fire should the Confederates break through.

Anna looked up and saw an injured Confederate soldier raise his musket at Martin, who knelt beside them. He was about to run him through. "Martin! Look out!" The musket came down and Martin moved aside at the last moment. He reached down and picked up a stray musket that was lying on the ground and blocked the soldier's second swing. Then a Union soldier put a pistol to the Confederate soldier's back and pulled the trigger.

"Get out of here boy!" The Union soldier shouted at Martin.

Stimulated with adrenaline, Martin grasped the musket tightly should any more Confederates draw near. Momentarily, the fighting began to ease around them.

"We're pushing them back," Martin announced to the three Johnstons. "The Confederates are retreating!" The Union soldiers cheered the Confederate's trumpet call to retreat.

Martin examined the rifle that he had picked up and handed it to Anna. "Here it is! Of all the rifles I could have picked up on this field, here is the one you were looking for. Here's your musket. What are the chances? It saved my life."

"What?" Anna took it out of his hands, and goose bumps rose up on both of her arms. She couldn't believe it! She looked at the butt of the stock and saw the name "Johnny."

"Whose name is this?"

"Mine," Martin announced.

Anna and Charity shared a confused glance. "But your name's Martin, right?" Charity asked.

"Johnny Martin Johnston. My parents called me by my middle name."

The three Johnstons exchanged a stunned glance. God was truly a God of miracles. This was their chance; they reached for the musket...

"But Daniel, he's not with us." Charity's fears were alleviated the moment that the three of them touched the musket at the same time.

The colors around them – blood-stained Confederate gray and Union royal blue from the uniforms of fallen warriors - shot up into the air like an explosion in a paint factory. The wall of color and texture began to swirl around them. They stood as the whirlwind began to pick up speed.

"Betcha that Johnny fella's freakin' out right now." James giggled at the thought.

"Hey, y'all!" The three Johnstons turned and saw their little brother standing next to him.

"Daniel!" they all shouted and clutched him, elated.

Daniel appeared stunned for a moment. "What happened?" He began to hug them one at a time. He looked into Charity's eyes. "I can't believe it! I was helpin' the master and all of a sudden, I was gone!"

"The master?" James wondered.

Charity smiled, and gave Daniel another hug. "I'm so glad you're okay."

Daniel's face contorted into a painful grimace, and he wiped his eyes with the back of his hands. "Oh, I pray my mother can be free soon - I mean, Eli's mother."

Charity's heart warmed as she recalled the godly wisdom of the African American slave woman. "She will. Righteousness and freedom are like two peas in a pod. They grow together."

James leaned in closer to Charity to be heard over the roar of the whirlwind all around them. "We found the rifle with Johnny's name on it. Does this mean we are going home now?"

"Yes, I think so." The rushing wind and spinning debris began to slowly subside. "We found Johnny's musket. He was a Johnston. Who'd a thunk it?"

James grabbed onto Charity's arm. "But what does that mean?"

"I don't know." Anna shook her head side to side. "But all things work together for the good, to them that love God, to them who are called according to His purpose."

"Oh God," Daniel prayed, "please send us home."

The whirlwind of colors began to slow and the debris gradually fell to the ground. They were relieved to find themselves on the same creek bed where they found the musket rifle what seemed like years ago.

But their relief was only temporary. It was Daniel who first noticed the changes. Something was different. Drastically different.

Chapter 7

"Where are the leaves?" Daniel asked. "And where's the water in the creek?"

When they left, the trees were clothed with the brightly colored red and yellow leaves of the Ohio fall, but now they were bare. The creek was all dried up. The erratically cracked white limestone base of the shallow, curvy creek was bone dry.

"And what's this?" Charity raised her right hand in which she had always held a weapon in their trips through time. But in her hand now was not an old rusty musket, but a book. It was a maroon Gideon Bible.

"Whoa!" James touched it, and turned it over, and they all stared in awe at the front cover of the Bible. It was identical to the Bible their family used for devotion for years; the front cover had been partially chewed by their dog Lucy one summer afternoon after devotions in the back yard.

Anna said what they all were thinking, "It's not over yet. This is our creek, but it's not over."

The ever-aware Daniel was the first to notice the line of smoke through the barren gray branches. It was coming from the direction of their home. He began running up the hill through their woods toward their home calling out, "Mom! Dad! Grace! Elijah! Faith!" He even called out for the blue-eyed dog that they rescued from the animal shelter. "Lucy! Where are you!?"

When they ran up the trail and into their back yard, they saw something that snatched their breath away. The four Johnstons stood in horror and watched their home engulfed in flames. They sprinted as close as they could to the house without risking getting burned by the flames. Billows of smoke flowed through the windows from the rooms where they once ate, slept, and played. Bursting into bitter tears, they all ran around the house, crying out for their brothers and sisters, desperately searching for any signs of their family.

When they had run completely around the house, they stopped to catch their breath. "What is happening?" Charity exclaimed between pitiful sobs. She bent down weeping and breathing heavily with her hands on her knees.

"We'll be all right." James wiped his tears, took a deep breath, and tried to be strong for his siblings. "Freaking out isn't a fruit of the Spirit. What did Dad and Mom always tell us was the first thing we should do when something bad happens?"

"Pray," they all said at the same time.

Charity broke out into a spontaneous prayer, her voice trembling with grief and fear. "Oh God, help us figure out what's going on. Help us find our family."

It was a moment later when they noticed that their neighbors' homes were completely burnt to the ground. Thin wisps of spoke ascended to heaven from the ash-filled debris.

"What in the world? Where is everybody?" Charity's tears continued to flow.

"Shouldn't there be fire trucks here by now?" Anna looked at the horizon with her hands shielding her eyes. "It's like a war zone."

"And look at the trees." Daniel pointed at the trees all around them. Trees that used to stand tall had been long cut down and uprooted. New trees had long ago been planted and were beginning to grow tall. The fruit trees in the front yard had been replaced with younger trees and the electric fence around the garden had been knocked down. The black plastic sheeting that covered the garden was rotted and remnants of it had been blown against the half-standing fence posts.

"Look!" Charity exclaimed. "The barn!" They ran to the barn where their two horses were housed and where the chickens and ducks nested, and they immediately realized that this was not the same barn. The structure was the same, but the paint was a different color, the base of the pole barn was rotted in several places. Their new barn looked ancient.

"But we found the musket with Johnny's name on it," Anna complained in a pitiful voice as she walked into a horse stall. "What's going on?"

"I don't know." Charity turned the pages of the maroon Bible, looking for any hints or clues as to why the weapon had turned into a Bible. "This is our house and our property, but we're in the future."

"Why don't we all touch the Bible now," Daniel proposed, "and maybe we can go home now."

"I don't think that'll work." Charity shut the Bible and sat on a ledge between the two stalls. "God brought us here for a reason and we won't leave until we've discovered it."

"Let's try," said Anna, touching the Bible at the same time as the others.

Nothing happened.

"I told you. We're on a mission from God, and we won't be able to get away from it anymore than Jonah could get away from preaching in Nineveh."

The first shot came right into the barn through the partially ajar door, and went between the girls and the boys, chilling them all to the bone. The bolt of blue light struck the ladder and the wall beside the ladder in the storage area of the barn. It burnt a perfectly round hole the size of a basketball in the wood. The sound of the shot was like a high-pitched squeal from a bad microphone in church.

"Ahhh!" cried several of them at the same time. The smell that filled their nostrils was like the smell of the air after a strong spring rain, except more intense.

"It was lightning!" Charity's facial features trembled.

Anna furrowed her brow. "Coming sideways?"

"And it's not storming," Daniel pointed out.

"No, it's not lightning." Lightning, James knew, didn't burn holes in wood that were perfectly circular. He touched the smoking edge of the hole in the wood, and then opened the door slightly with his other hand. What he saw made the color drain from his rosy cheeks. It was a hovering aircraft, about five feet in diameter and two feet high. It was shaped like a small car, and emitted some kind of heat underneath it. Three bent rods projected toward the ground from the aircraft's belly.

"Run!" James slammed the door shut and jumped the waist-high wall between the storage area and the horse stall and his three siblings followed close behind. "It's some kind of remote-controlled airplane!"

When they came out of the horse stall into the fenced-in field, the hovering aircraft floated around the side of the barn facing the home. It again fired a speeding bolt of blue light at them, just missing James. His nose burned with the pungent smell that emanated from the weapon.

"Back into the barn!" They jumped over the wall separating the horse stall from the storage area, and went back out the door just as the aircraft fired another burst at the door, burning a large hole in it.

They ducked on the side of the barn facing the woods, hoping the cover of the branches overhead would provide them some protection. James kept his ear to the door of the barn, listening carefully, and when he heard the aircraft back out of the stall and go back around the side of the barn facing the home, he whispered to his siblings, "Draw it back around the front of the barn. I'll climb into the hay loft and when it crosses that large window facing the field…"

"What are you going to do?" Anna asked worriedly.

"Destroy it," James whispered.

"With what?"

"Just do it." James opened the door of the barn and quietly went up the ladder to the hayloft.

Charity pushed Anna and Daniel into the chicken coop, shut the door, and then went around the far side of the barn. If she could draw the aircraft across the window in front of the barn, then that would give James a chance.

When the aircraft rounded the back of the barn, it saw Charity's shadow and calculated she was on the other side. It came low to the ground and Charity, hearing its hum, tiptoed to the front of the barn and got ready to run. As soon as it came around the corner, it rose over the wooden fence and fired another shot at Charity. She darted across the front of the barn and the laser left a long black streak in the dirt, melting sand to black glass.

The hovering aircraft picked up speed and as it crossed under the large window, James jumped out of the window holding a shovel above his head with both hands. He swung it down and whacked the top of the hovering aircraft with a loud "Hyah!"

When the shovel collided with the hovering aircraft, sparks flew and singed James' skin. He managed to land on his feet in the soft ground and, other than a few superficial burns, was not hurt.

The hovering aircraft lost its equilibrium and began to spin erratically across the field, shooting its laser bursts in different directions. James dove into one of the horse stalls to avoid being struck. The aircraft spun sideways, flipped upside down, and came crashing into the ground. A huge ball of blue flames shot up into the air and then a loud noise like thunder shook the ground beneath their feet.

"Whoa!" said Daniel as he and Anna stepped out of the chicken coop. "What was that?"

"Good job, James!" Charity walked up to him and helped him to his feet. "That was some kind of flying tank or something."

"With a powerful weapon on it." Anna wiped the sweat off her brow. "You all right, James?"

"Yeah." James had mud on his face from diving into the horse stall. He wiped his face and looked more closely at the small burn marks on his forearms. "It burns, but not too bad."

"You're amazing!" Daniel praised him.

James grinned widely, and flexed his biceps. "With arms like these, you have to be *really* humble." The girls laughed at their little brother when Daniel made a frantic announcement that made their hair stand on end.

"There's another one!" Their hearts dropped into their stomachs as they looked at the horizon across the field. "No, two more coming!" Daniel pointed at two hovering aircraft low to the ground, speeding directly toward them.

"Make for the woods!" Charity shouted as they ran around the barn, jumped the fence, and sprinted into the thicket. Thorns cut into their skin, but they kept running, their lives on the line. Two laser pulses whizzed by their heads, the blue lights cutting down trees and branches as it passed by them. Then, in front of them, they saw what looked like two different colored lasers firing right at them. These laser pulses were red and more narrow than the large caliber bolts of blue light that were fired from the ominous hovering aircrafts. These two bursts of red lasers from an unknown location in the woods made the Johnstons drop to the ground. There was nowhere left to run. They heard two explosions from behind them, and then two loud bangs of thunder that shook the ground. Someone in the woods had taken out the two hovering aircraft.

The Johnstons slowly stood and breathed a sigh of relief. Their eyes searched the woods for whomever it was that had saved their lives. Two men wearing camouflaged pants and shirts and green and black face paint stepped out of the bushes and started walking up to them. "You guys okay?"

"Yeah." Anna wiped her nose, as it appeared to burn from the strong smell that emanated from the blue laser pulses. "That was close." She lifted her arm and saw that the burst of laser from one of the aircraft had just skimmed her and burnt part of her shirt black.

"That's some gun." James motioned toward the weapons that the two men carried. Their rifles looked like his Dad's AR-15, except with a wider barrel.

Charity studied the two young men for a moment, finding them strangely familiar in spite of their face paint. "Who are you?"

"I'm Israel, he's Joseph." The tallest and youngest of the two massaged his thick, brown beard. "What are y'all doing out here?"

"That's our home." Anna pointed at the burning house. "That was our barn, but it looks different now. Where are our horses?"

The two men looked at each other, perplexed. Joseph, the more aged-looking and shorter of the two said, "My parents used to live there before the war."

"Before the war?"

"Yeah. They got out just before the 'arleys' started taking out the homes of suspected militia."

"What an 'arley'?" wondered Anna.

"R-L-E-H, which stands for Remote Laser-equipped Hovercrafts. We just call them arleys." Joseph's gaze shifted suspiciously between the four young kids. "Say, where have y'all been for the last five years?"

"Oh, here and there." Charity pointed in the direction of one of their neighbors whose home was in charred ruins. "Were our neighbors militia too?"

"Those homes have been long ago abandoned. With the dropping birthrate for so many decades, lots of homes are abandoned now. The arleys take them out just in case the militia are hiding there."

"So your parents used to live in our house, huh? What are the names of your parents?"

"Elijah and Yoshibell Johnston."

Charity, Anna, James, and Daniel could not believe their ears. All at once they realized that the older of these two men was the son of their little brother Elijah.

Just to be sure, Anna asked, "Who are Elijah's parents?"

"Patrick and Elizabeth, of course. How would you know them? They've been dead for a long time."

"Mom and Dad are dead?" Daniel rubbed his eyes with the back of his hands, choked up with grief.

Charity placed her hand on Daniel's shoulder. "It's all right, Daniel. It's not what you think." She looked at Joseph. "Tell me, sir, what year is this?"

"It's the year 2085. What year did you think it was?"

James knew that the quickest way out of this nightmare was to figure out why God sent them 75 years into the future. "Tell us about the war, Joseph."

"First, let's go deeper into the cover of the woods. The cloud cover is thin. The satellites can see us here." Joseph cast a careful glance at the cloudy skies above them, then turned and headed into the thicket.

The Johnstons followed the two men deep into the woods.

"Is that a Bible?" the taller of the two young men asked Charity. His eyes were fixed on the hardback maroon book she held in her right hand.

"Yeah. What's your name again?"

"Israel. Israel Zastrow."

All four Johnstons exclaimed at the same time, "Zastrow?"

"Yeah," Israel said with a wide grin. He looked over his shoulder at the four kids who followed him down the deer trail. "Are we that famous?"

"Of course!" Daniel laughed and slapped his thigh. "Your Dad used to give us the funnest bear rides."

"Bear rides?"

"Not real bear rides. They were pretend."

"You know my dad?"

"Of course we know him. Cal Zastrow was one of our favorite missionaries."

"Cal's not my dad, he's my grandpa. He died on the mission field years ago."

"Oh. I keep forgetting what year it is."

Joseph and Israel looked over their shoulders at the four strange kids that followed them through the woods.

"What's up with these guys?" Israel whispered to Joseph.

"I don't know." Joseph shrugged. "Maybe the brush with the arleys messed with their heads."

"Grandpa did give us some fun rides on his back. I remember those," Israel reminisced with a grin that pressed the limits of his face. "But I don't see how you would know him. He's been gone to heaven since before you were born."

"Tell us about the war," James asked. "Who were those hovercrafts fighting for?"

"Ohio was one of a dozen states that banned abortion, physician-assisted suicide, and gay marriage, and declared its sovereignty. We defied the federal judges' unlawful decisions, and when the feds retaliated and sent FBI guards to keep the killing centers open and hand out marriage licenses to gays, Dad fought 'em."

"You mean Elijah Johnston?"

"Yeah. He's in charge now."

"Is he the governor?"

"We haven't had a governor since the capital of Ohio was destroyed by terrorists last year. But Elijah was the Speaker of the House, and he's one of the few surviving legislators. He's been keeping a government together, mostly that just does justice for the people and resists tyranny."

"Right on." Charity flipped up both of her thumbs at her siblings, and they responded in kind.

Joseph Johnston looked back at Charity. "Can I hold your Bible?"

Charity smiled. "Sure." She extended it toward him and he took it gently in his hands. He patted both covers, and then opened it up ever so gently to one of his favorite psalms. "You act like you've never seen one before."

"Oh, I saw one a couple of years ago."

"What?" Anna was shocked.

Charity's eyes widened and her mouth gaped open. The four

Johnstons found that hard to believe. "You mean you haven't seen a Bible is two years?"

"Not since the feds outlawed them in their Tolerance Act, and the public schools and public libraries started destroying them. I used to read one on-line before the feds shut down the Internet. A couple of my uncles have put together a printing press and they should be printing Bibles any day now. But most people are scared to own a Bible due to the penalties if the feds catch them."

Joseph handed the Bible back to Charity and she carried it with more care than she did before. "Tell us what Elijah's been doing to resist the federal government?"

Joseph sighed, as if he didn't want to think about it. He finally answered: "Dad started just arresting people who tried to abort babies, but when the feds banned guns and when socialism started causing the economy to sink like the Titanic, Ohio was one of several states that finally seceded and kicked out the feds. Then, it got real nasty real fast. The feds invaded, demolished half our Guard forces, stopped all government money coming into Ohio, and set up a blockade around us. We've got a strong militia now, and we're well armed, but our economy is in chaos. We can trade with Kentucky, who is one of the dozen righteous states, but our other borders are well guarded. All those who have been dependent on the feds for food, healthcare, housing, education, and other handouts have been rioting and fighting us. I think we're reaching a breaking point."

"A breaking point?" Charity wondered.

"Yeah." Joseph and Israel shared a troubled glance. "Dad's considering a peace treaty. As a matter of fact, he plans on signing it tomorrow. The feds will let us open our borders for trade and will resume Social Security payments and healthcare coverage for all Ohioans if we re-join the Union."

"And they promise not to prosecute our leaders," Israel added.

Anna chuckled. "And you believe them? You know that the feds will start killing babies again."

"Babies are dying anyway in back alley abortions. And the feds will let us ban abortion in most cases. It's a positive step toward peace."

"*Most* cases?" Charity blurted out. "You're going to let them kill *some* babies *with* your permission because they're killing some babies *without* your permission? Being an accomplice in mass murder is not a positive step toward peace, my friend. And why would you call that a peace treaty anyway? It's not that peaceful for the babies."

The two young men looked back at Charity, and appeared offended at her critique. Joseph shook his head and made eye contact with her. "You just don't know what we've been through."

"You've got a righteous cause," said Anna, "and you've been doing justice like the Bible says. God will help you if you will be faithful. Why are you giving up?"

Joseph's face reddened. "Ohio's in chaos. There's lots of rioting, anarchy, and infighting. We're just trying to make the best of a bad situation."

James patted Joseph on the shoulder. "You didn't expect it to be easy to get to the Promised Land, did you?"

Daniel nodded. "I'm sure that giving up was not something your parents and grandparents taught you. Looks like not having a Bible has hurt you more than you realize. The Bible says that there is no restraint to the Lord to save by many or by few."

Now, the four Johnstons could tell that Israel Zastrow and Joseph Johnston were upset, by the way the back of their ears got red and they developed a more rigid posture to their gait. They walked on quietly for a moment until Charity broke the uneasy silence.

"We need to see your dad, Joseph. We need to see him before he signs that treaty."

"He's in Zanesville today – thankfully not at his home when it was destroyed by the feds. You just might get to meet him."

"I'm sure he'd like to meet you four." Israel turned and winked at Joseph, who nodded and grunted.

Charity put her arms over her siblings' shoulders as they all prayed quietly. They were beginning to realize God's purpose in sending them to so many battles in the past: He did it so that they could learn from them and impact the future. History is "His story" and history is full of critical lessons too often unlearned. The losses and victories of men and civilizations throughout history can give us the key to conquering today's enemies and achieving victory in today's battles.

When they arrived at the home where Elijah was staying, they were told he was on the phone. This allowed them to get to know many of those who were in Elijah's inner circle. They met many brave warriors for Jesus Christ, fearless evangelists, bold Bible-smugglers, persecuted pastors and missionaries, mature patriarchs, guards carrying large black guns, and Spirit-filled statesmen. They were men and women of prayer, renown in heaven, well respected by Christians and thoroughly despised by communists and devils all over the world.

They also discovered that Elijah's wife was one of Cal and Trish Zastrow's kids. Did the Zastrows have a daughter named Yoshibell? They did not, so they speculated that the Zastrows must have adopted a child later in life.

Joseph poked his head out of Elijah's office and had washed the camouflaged paint from his face. He summoned the Johnston four. "Dad's ready for you now."

They knew it was Elijah the moment they laid their eyes on him. They gasped in wonder as if they were witnessing a miracle in progress. It was not what was different about Elijah that astounded them. His hair was now gray-white, his face criss-crossed with deep wrinkles, his clothes were well-worn, and his hands as thoroughly calloused as you'd expect a hard-working 78 year-old man's to be. It was what had remained since three-years-of-age that amazed them. With his dimpled smile, his buoyant curls, and his bright blue eyes underneath a crop of long, dark eyelashes, they knew it was him immediately. Charity wanted to go throw her arms around him, greet him with a kiss, and poke him in the belly button, but she knew that would be inappropriate.

He was on the phone when they entered the room that he used as a temporary office. His voice was hoarse from decades of faithful preaching and standing for righteousness in the public square. The old man waved them to some chairs in the corner of the room until he finished his conversation.

"Have the Guard on stand-by just in case." Elijah paused to listen intently. "I know we can't trust them, but we don't have a choice. All right? Update me tonight. Good bye." He closed his satellite cell phone and walked up to the four young children and introduced himself.

"Elijah Hudson Johnston." His smile was toothy, but warm and authentic.

178

"It's so good to meet you, Mr. Johnston." Charity stepped forward and shook the old man's hand, with the three younger Johnstons following her lead.

"Please, call me Elijah. My son Joseph tells me that we're related somehow, and you sure do bear some resemblance." He squinted as he studied them. "But my eyesight's failing me nowadays and my

glasses were in my home when the feds destroyed it. I'm kind of confused as to how we're related."

"That's understandable," Charity responded.

"Do you know what happened to your brothers?" James drew near to a photograph on a shelf that showed a picture with him as a young man next to several men and women in Arab garb.

"Yeah," said Daniel. "Especially James and Daniel."

"And who did Anna marry?" Anna asked.

"Well, let me think." Elijah massaged his gray beard with his hand as he mused on the answers to those questions.

"Uh, no, I'm sorry sir." Charity leaned toward Anna, James, and Daniel and whispered, "I don't think it's God's will for us to know personal stuff about who we marry and how we die."

"Why not?" James wondered.

"No, she's right," said Anna, nodding. "It's not natural."

James smiled and stretched out his hands. "None of this is natural."

"It's supernatural," Daniel observed.

James pulled out of Charity's huddle and made eye contact with the old man. "Can you at least tell me if James died a martyr on the mission field?"

Charity squealed, "No James!"

But it was too late. Elijah nodded in response to the question and James thrust a fist into the air. "Yes!"

Charity snarled at him in disappointment, and then James smiled at her. "Don't worry. It doesn't hurt. I had a dream about it."

Elijah stepped closer to the four. "My sister Charity's married to the–"

"Please stop!" Charity blurted out. She felt guilty for interrupting the old man and respectfully apologized to him. "I'm sorry, but we don't want to hear anything else about our future."

"*Your* future?" Elijah had a puzzled look on his wrinkled face.

"The future of Patrick and Elizabeth Johnston's kids, I mean. We have more import-ant things to talk about."

A 12-year-old young lady suddenly walked into the room that took their breath away. She brought a platter with five cups of tea on it, and five muffins. She was absolutely beautiful, with an appearance that mimicked their five-year-old sister Grace with big blue eyes, golden hair full of curls, a flawless complexion, and full, pink lips.

"Who are you?" Anna's eyes were fixed upon her as she passed around her cups of tea and homemade muffins.

"Hope Anne's my name."

"Are you related to Grace Johnston, you know, the daughter of Patrick and Elizabeth?"

"That's my grandmother. How'd you know that?"

Daniel grinned ear to ear. "Wow! You look just like her."

"That's what people tell all fifteen of her kids."

"Fifteen? Little Gracie had fifteen kids?"

"Yep." When her platter was empty she headed out of the room. "Though I don't think anybody calls her Little Gracie anymore."

She laughed as she walked through the door.

Elijah came and sat in a chair beside them. Charity turned to the old man and sighed deeply. He had a busy day and only promised them ten minutes of his time, so she came right to the point. She raised her maroon Bible toward him. "Elijah, do you recognize this?"

Elijah reached for it and took it into his hands. He massaged its cover and his aged eyes appeared to brighten as he went back in time. "Where in the world did you get this?"

"There's a long story to that, but if you permit me, I'd like to share a verse with you out of its pages." Charity reached for the Bible and he reluctantly handed it back to her.

"*You* want to share a verse with *me*?" His voice was heavy with skepticism and doubt. These were kids, and he had more important things to do than receive counsel from children. He glanced at his watch, and Charity grew concerned that Elijah would not be receptive to what they had to say.

"Lord, open his heart," she prayed quietly as she opened her Bible.

Suddenly, loud sirens resounded throughout the house. They were so loud that they made the Johnston kids put their hands over their ears. The two young men who saved them from the hovering aircrafts rushed into the room. "Everyone to the bomb shelter! James and Daniel, you come with me. We'll guard the perimeter. Go, go, go!"

Elijah grabbed Charity and Anna's hands and fled with them to a side exit, where they descended some steps and went through a heavy iron door and into a cool, dark room. Elijah stood at the entrance while all of the women and children in the home flooded into the room. One of the ladies flipped a light switch and turned on a machine that sputtered to life and began to hum quietly. This device allowed them to breathe oxygen and shut out the gas that the feds might shoot into the home during an attack.

Charity stopped Elijah from shutting the door. "No. Anna and I can fight."

Elijah put up his palm, oblivious to her confidence. "Women under fifteen stay in the cellar with me. No exceptions. If our boys can't repel them, we'll be fighting for our lives soon enough. We have the most important job in here anyway."

"Really? What's that?" Anna wondered.

"We pray." Elijah shut and locked the door and began to counsel them all: "Pray! Pray as if the lives of your husbands, sons, and fathers depended on it." Then he lifted his eyes and both of his hands toward heaven, and everybody in the room simultaneously began to implore the King of heaven for help.

* * * * *

James and Daniel followed the men to the front porch, their hands sheltering their ears from the loud siren that blared overhead. Dozens of other men and women scurried past them toward their stations around the home when the two men turned to the brothers.

"Take these." Israel Zastrow, the young, tall man with the baby face and the brown beard handed Daniel and James two gas masks to put on. "Put them on like me." The two Johnston boys put the small black masks over their mouth, nose, and eyes, and pulled the strap over the back of their heads. Israel touched a button on the sides of the masks that caused a seal to be made in the mask.

"Take a deep breath." James and Daniel did as he said, and a cool influx of fresh air entered the mask. "This is just in case they use gas."

Joseph Johnston, the middle-aged fellow with the red beard, checked his battery power gauge on the side of his gun. He extended the gun to James. "Do you two know how to shoot?"

"Yeah." James took the gun out of Joseph's hand. "But we never shot one of these."

"Here's the safety," Joseph said, pointing. "Just point and shoot. Your energy's good for at least a few thousand pulses." The gun felt light, and for a moment James thought it was a toy gun. "It's impossible to shoot yourself or anything else within one meter. It's a safety precaution. But they're very deadly beyond that up to 1000 meters. Be careful."

Israel handed a gun to Daniel. "Here's yours."

"Thanks."

James and Daniel followed Joseph and Israel into the back yard and took cover behind a pile of firewood next to an old rusty go-cart.

Joseph opened his cell phone, and a colorful display shone on it. It was a satellite image of their location. He spoke into a microphone affixed to his gas mask, and redeployed some men to another side of the home. Young men and women rushed to and fro, getting into position for the coming onslaught.

Israel Zastrow tapped the gas tank on the old rusty go-cart three times.

"Whatcha doing that for?" James asked.

Suddenly, the seat of the go-cart raised into the air, revealing a trap door.

"Whoa!"

Joseph answered James' question. "That leads to the interceptors." Israel descended the ladder of the trap door and the go-cart's seat came back down and sealed around the opening.

"Interceptors? What are those?"

"They intercept the bombs after they are released. It's like a speeding bullet taking out another speeding bullet, but they're pretty accurate. They can even take out jets that are overhead and close to us."

As they spoke, a circular patch of grass flipped upside down and a metal tube as big around as a cup arose out of the ground two feet in front of the rusty go-cart. It immediately released two bright orange laser bursts into the air, which whistled into the cloudy sky. The sirens ceased and all was quiet for a moment.

Joseph knelt behind the pile of wood and studied the horizon with his scope. Daniel and James gazed into the sky overhead, white with a thick layer of clouds. "I don't hear any jets. Where are the bad guys?"

"Sometimes they fly their jets in the stratosphere and you can't see them until they fly straight down on top of you. And they are almost completely silent. Other times they will employ hovercrafts that approach so close to the ground you cannot see them well in this wooded hilly country until they're already shooting at you."

"Here they come." A young man to their right, who leaned against a large oak tree and studied the forest with his powerful riflescope, pointed at the horizon and repeated, "Here they come." They saw several hovercrafts coming right at them. The blue lasers started firing at them in rapid secession, instantly killing several of the men. The laser bursts that missed them put holes in the brick house behind them. The warriors around them returned fire, sending their red laser pulses over the hills and into the woods.

Two more orange laser bolts were fired into the cloudy sky from another interceptor on the other side of the home.

As laser bursts exploded trees and stone and incinerated flesh, James and Daniel just clung low to the ground. When they witnessed the courage of the men who defended their leader and their freedom, they poked their heads above the pile of wood and began to return fire. They were amazed at the destructive power of these weapons, and the lack of kick when they pulled the trigger.

"Got one!" Daniel exclaimed.

"I got one too!" James fired again, causing a hovercraft to explode in a ball of blue flames.

Daniel saw it and hollered, "Good shot!"

The thunderous bang of the hovercrafts exploding shook the leaves off some of the trees.

A moment later, they heard, "All clear!" The thirteenth

remote-controlled, laser-equipped hovercraft had been destroyed, and a cheer of victory went up that reminded them of the cheers of victory they heard at the valley of Elah, the Battle of Tours, and the Battles of Lexington and Gettysburg. The surviving warriors began to assist the wounded and take count of the dead, whereas Joseph Johnston opened his cell phone to make a phone call. The home behind them was as full of holes as a block of swiss cheese. The black holes smoked and weakened the structure of the home, and part of the roof collapsed.

"Shhh! Quiet!" said Joseph. "Hear that?"

James turned his ear to the sky. "I don't hear anything."

Joseph spoke into his cell. "Call you back." Then he touched a button on his cell and studied the colorful display that revealed to him that two manned aircraft, which had been shot out of the sky by their underground interceptors, were falling right toward them. "Take cover! Take cover!"

Joseph fell to the ground with the Johnston boys and he began to pray, "Lord, don't let it hit the house." James and Daniel joined him in the prayer and then heard the rumble, as if it were an oncoming train. It got louder and louder until it sounded like it was right on top of them.

The two small jets struck the ground in front of them about a hundred feet away. They collided with such force that the dirt underneath their feet trembled as if an earthquake had struck. A huge cloud of dirt and smoke obscured the sky. Momentarily, when the dust began to settle, Joseph looked at the bright display on his cell phone and called out, "All clear!"

Another victory shout went out and James and Daniel put their weapons on safety and high-fived each other. Joseph again studied the reading on his cell phone. "I think we're okay, for now. That was weird."

The look on his face concerned James. "What?"

Israel ascended from the underground bunker underneath the go-cart, and he immediately echoed Joseph's concern. "Something's not right."

Now, James and Daniel grew uneasy. They flicked the button on their weapons to return them to firing position, and James even began to study the horizon again with his scope. "What's not right?

Please, tell me."

"That was too easy."

James looked back at Joseph. "Too easy?"

"They wouldn't risk an attack on the eve of signing the treaty unless they were sending a stronger force to completely overwhelm us. It doesn't make sense. Maybe it was a diversion."

"To divert us from what?"

Joseph shrugged and tapped a button on the phone. "Squad one and three, keep watch at your position. Everybody else, retreat to the house and prepare for re-deployment. We've got to find another location."

* * * * *

The 78-year-old Elijah heard a tap on the door of the cellar. His three-year-old great grandson held tight to his leg with one arm and grasped a plastic green water gun with his other.

"Great grandpa, is it over?"

"I don't know, son."

"Are you gonna open the door?"

"In a minute."

When it was quiet for several minutes, Elijah assumed that the battle had concluded and that they were safe. He heard another tap on the iron door. He cracked the door and saw something he did not expect.

A toaster rested on the ground in front of the door. Just a plain old toaster. Elijah called out, "Joseph? Israel? Are you there?"

Elijah did not see the beady, metallic robot eyes protrude from the two slits in the top of the toaster. He looked up the stairwell for any signs of life. "Anybody there?" He paused and listened, but didn't hear the faint hum the strange toaster emitted. "That's strange—"

Suddenly, the robotic toaster began to float into the air and the knob in front of the toaster protruded and became a miniature laser gun aimed at Elijah's head.

"It's a Kill-Bot!" Elijah tried to slam the iron door shut but the Kill-Bot was too fast, and stuck one of its robot arms into the door to keep it cracked. It fired an electric bolt of lightning into the room, which skimmed Elijah's head and disintegrated a curl of his white-gray hair.

"Ow!" The bolt shocked him, but he managed to keep pressing against the door to keep the Kill-Bot from entering. "Hide! Quick!"

Little Hope Anne pulled Charity and Anna away from the door. "Come with me."

"But we've got to save Elijah!" Anna pulled her hand out of Hope Anne's grasp. "He needs our—" Anna's sentence was cut short by an electric bolt that was fired through the crack in the door. The bolt skimmed her leg and knocked her five feet across a meticulously stacked pile of applesauce-filled mason jars. Her body slammed against the wall and she fell to the ground unconscious, smoke emanating from her knee.

"Anna!" Charity jumped to Anna's side and bent down to her. Anna was motionless, her eyes frozen open, staring into space. "She's not breathing!"

Hope Anne bent down beside Charity, raised a fist high in the air, and brought it down against Anna's chest with a "Thud." Charity became upset: "What'd you do that for?" Charity's complaint was cut short by a blast of lightning that whizzed by her head, making her dizzy. The Kill-Bot could not see into the room and was firing blindly.

Hope Anne's fist against Anna's chest caused Anna's heart to beat again. She sat up coughing, and Charity pulled her back to the ground. They crawled behind a stack of canned vegetables against the wall.

"Get the water guns!" Elijah shouted.

"Water guns?" Charity wondered.

"They're our only defense against the Kill-Bots," Hope Anne said. "They have a laser shield, but water shorts them out and paralyzes them." Charity and Anna had confused looks on their faces, so Hope Anne added, "Made in China with parts from North Korea, and assembled in Cuba."

"Oh."

Everybody scurried to the top of the shelves to get their water guns.

The Kill-Bot increased the power to the engines that caused it to hover in the air, and Elijah could no longer hold the door shut. "I can't hold it anymore!" He suddenly let go of the door and jumped behind a row of bottled water.

The Kill-Bot was thrown off balance by the sudden release of the door and went into the room, hovering erratically as it tried to focus on its target, which was the elderly Elijah Johnston.

As the Kill-Bot hovered, looking for a place to aim its two weapons, a thin stream of water came from the top of the shelf next to it and bolts of lightning emitted from its robotic eyes, causing the water jugs next to it to explode and spray drops of water all over the room.

A suspenseful moment of silence followed.

Elijah broke the silence. "Clear!" They all stepped out from behind the shelves where they hid, and saw Elijah's three-year-old grandchild standing on top of the shelf emitting a yellow stream from between his legs.

"Don't wook, I'm not done!" he said, embarrassed.

"What do you think you're doing?" Elijah steadied his grandson's legs so he wouldn't fall.

"There wadn't any wadder in my wadder gun," he said. "I dwank it all."

"Good job, little Johnny. Good job!"

* * * * *

Young men packed Elijah's laptops and books into boxes. Women scurried about transporting food and kitchen supplies into styrofoam coolers. They packed the goods into the trunks of cars and the back of trucks in preparation for relocation. Elijah sat down with the four Johnstons to give them their promised opportunity to speak with him. They sipped on small porcelain cups of Hope Anne's famous mint tea.

"We have to keep moving because they're always attacking," Elijah said between blows onto his steaming cup.

"Your men defended you well." James waved at the last young man to leave the room with two heavy boxes under his arms.

"You should have seen Elijah's great grandchild little Johnny in the cellar." Charity looked at Anna and they laughed at the thought of him.

"Johnny?" James had a look of surprise on his face. "You found our 'Johnny'?"

"Yep," she said with a smile, "he's a Johnny."

"And he saved the day," Anna added.

"Man," James blew out a noisy breath of air as he wagged his head, "I'm namin' all my kids Johnny. Johnny 1, Johnny 2, Johnny 3..." The Johnstons all shared a hearty laugh.

When it was silent, Charity added, "Johnny 13, Johnny 14, Johnny 15..."

They laughed again, and James nodded. "Yep. Havin' too many kids is like havin' too many blessings. It's not possible."

"God has always defended us well." The elderly Elijah's eyes glanced heavenward, as if praying a prayer of thanksgiving to their protector and defender.

"So why would the feds launch an attack on you the day before you're scheduled to sign a peace treaty with them?" Anna scratched her head, perplexed by the apparent contradiction.

"I suppose if they kill me before I sign it, then they can win without having to compromise anything."

"But how can you trust them to keep their promises anyway?" Charity picked up the maroon Bible that sat on the nightstand beside her. "If they're willing to kill babies and elderly people and attack you with weapons of war without a good reason, how can you trust them to not prosecute Ohio's leaders after you've turned your government over to them?"

Elijah sighed and looked down, the wrinkles on his face lengthening at Charity's words. "I don't trust them. Not at all. But some parts of Ohio's big cities are filled with anarchy and crime. Too many people are dependent on the government to care for them. They have no thirst for the liberty that's found in Christ. They have no hunger for the adventure of self-government."

"All those are reasons you should trust God and do *more* justice, not retreat and give up." James leaned forward in his chair with his elbows on his knees. "Satan's upset. So what? Greater is He who is in you than he that is in the world. You are more than a conqueror through Him that loves you. Right?"

Elijah sat back in his chair and crossed his arms over his chest as he carefully considered the admonition. He appeared as if he were studying the design of the cheap Persian rug on which their chairs and couches rested, but in truth, he was praying silently, trying to hear God's voice.

"You can't sign that treaty tomorrow." Charity was adamant. "You just can't! God will defend you if you trust Him." She extended her maroon Gideon Bible toward him. "You know what this book says. 'Blessed is the nation whose God is the Lord.' Why on earth would you want to submit to an evil government and risk losing God's blessing? You'd come under judgment. Stand fast therefore in the liberty wherewith Christ has made you free, and be not entangled again in the yoke of bondage. Be excellent at good and innocent of evil, and the God of peace shall soon crush Satan under your feet." She waved the book above her head as she spoke.

"Amen," the other Johnstons responded simultaneously.

Elijah reached for the Bible and Charity gave it to him. He turned it over in his hands, and then opened it up to the reference from which Charity quoted, Psalm 33:12. He sighed deeply, letting the truth of God's Word soak into his heart as he massaged its cardboard binding with his calloused fingers.

"Elijah, listen to me." He looked up at the voice and his eyes fastened upon James. "If you bow down to the federal government because you doubt God will meet your needs, how's that different from Israel believing the ten false spies and disbelieving the two true spies at the foot of the Jordan River?"

Elijah stood to his feet. "I don't have a choice! Over half of Ohio is fighting me, the rightful leader. Many Ohioans are starving. The feds are forcing the banks to foreclose on them and they're losing their homes and being kicked out on the street, being left at the mercy of federally funded gangs of drug-dealers and criminals let out of prison early for good behavior. Businesses are leaving Ohio and people are losing their jobs. We *must* make peace."

Anna took a deep breath as Elijah sat back down. "But at what cost, Elijah? Are you going to make peace with evil leaders at the cost of the lives of Ohio's preborn babies and elderly grandparents? You're going to give up their lives and surrender your freedom so that you can have more jobs and keep your homes? Is that a cost you're willing to pay for a Social Security check? A little communism for a little candy? Please! It'd be like the nation of Israel trying to make peace with the Philistines the day before David was going to impale a stone into the forehead of Goliath. It'd be like Charles Martel throwing in the towel on the day before their victory at the Battle of Tours."

James nodded. "Or it'd be like Sam Adams giving up in Boston and making peace with Britain when the redcoats invaded. You've got to stand your ground on the Word and give God a chance to show Himself strong."

Daniel spoke up: "One thing I've learned in the hard times I've been through is that you shouldn't be afraid. If you will trust God and step into the water, you'll either walk on the water or God'll split the Red Sea for you. Faith is the victory that overcomes the world. It's unbelief that destroys nations, from Israel to the long list of Gentile nations that have crumbled in anarchy, tyranny, and chaos."

Elijah appeared deep in thought. He massaged his chin and a tear came to his eye. "God is so good to me. He's such a patient and gentle friend. Whenever I stray a little from the path to which He has called me, He's always there to gently prod this stubborn lamb back onto the right trail."

"So you're not going to sign the treaty?" Charity asked hopefully.

Elijah shook his head and bit his lip. "How can I? My counselors are divided on the subject, and I think that I've been influenced by the cowardly half. I thank you for encouraging me to keep my sights set on God, and not on the enemy, and not even on Ohio. Thank you."

"You're welcome." Charity smiled at her brothers and her sister. "Let's go home." They drew near and prepared to all touch the Bible at the same time. Before they did, Charity told the 78-year-old Elijah, "No King but King Jesus!"

Elijah stood to his feet, thrust both of his fists into the air and with a huge smile on his face, shouted, "No King but King Jesus!"

"We love you, little brother."

* * * * *

The red, green, and brown colors of the Persian rug underneath their feet exploded into the air and began to swirl around them. The four Johnstons huddled together, wondering what in the world Elijah was thinking when they suddenly disappeared from his presence.

"God, I pray he didn't have a heart attack when he saw that," James prayed with a grin.

"Are we going home now?" asked Daniel.

Charity hugged Daniel close. "We'll go home when God's ready for us to go home. Who knows what adventure's next?"

The whirlwind gradually slowed and they each blacked out at the same time. Momentarily, they woke up, their legs and backs covered in black, wet soil. They rubbed their eyes, wondering what had just happened to them. In their trips through time, they had never before lost consciousness. They lay on their backs on the creek bed in the woods behind their house. Charity held the old rusty musket in her hands, the very same one that had the inscription "Johnny" on it.

"Are we home?" Daniel sat up, his eyes full of hope.

James put his forearms on his knees as he studied their surroundings. The trees were colored with the rich, deep colors of Ohio's fall. Rays of the sun pierced the trees, casting a kaleidoscope of colors onto them. "I think we're home."

Anna stuck her fingers in her ears and opened her mouth wide. "My ears are ringing. What happened?"

Charity looked down. Right in the middle of them all, they found a big black spot right in the center of the ground. It was still smoking when she reached over and touched a solitary leaf that hung from a waste high bush. When she touched it, it reduced to ash. "What in the world? Lightning struck the ground here."

"Maybe it hit the musket while we were all touching it." Anna struggled to her feet and brushed the mud off of her skirt.

Charity grasped tightly to the rusty musket, flipping it over and looking at it from all sides. "Did you guys have the same dream I had? Were we really there with David and Goliath, at the fall of Jerusalem in A.D. 70? Were we really at the battle of Tours, at Lexington and Gettysburg? Did we really talk with Elijah when he was an old man?"

They all three nodded.

James climbed to his feet with a grunt and then helped Charity and Daniel stand. "It couldn't have been a dream. How can we all have had the same dream at the same time?"

"Elijah was married to someone named Yoshibell Zastrow," Charity recalled. "The Zastrows don't even have a child named Yoshibell, and I don't think they can have any more kids."

They all heard her voice at the same time, and their hair stood on end.

"It's time for dinner!"

Oh, what a beautiful sound it was, like the sound of splashing water to a man about to die of thirst. Yet now, finally, the water was within reach. Their precious mother called out to them again at the top of her voice from the back porch. "It's time for dinner!"

"Yeah!" They began to race toward home, tears of joy filling their eyes. They had been gone for such a long time.

Elijah, Grace, and baby Faith were playing on the swing set. Charity and James stopped to play with them and tell them about their exciting dream. They were so happy to see their little brother and their little sisters again. As Charity showed them the rusty musket and told Elijah how he was famously used of God in their dream, she had the eerie feeling that, even if it was all just a dream, God was teaching them a lesson that they were going to need to remember.

Anna and Daniel bypassed the swing set and rushed up the back porch and into the kitchen to embrace their mother. Anna cried as she hugged her tightly.

"What's the matter? Are you okay?" Her mother dried her hands with a maroon towel and knelt down before Anna.

"I just missed you so, so much."

"You've only been gone for an hour." Her mother wiped her tears and hugged her again.

"You wouldn't believe what happened to us!" Daniel shouted as he also clutched his mother tightly.

"Not so loud." His mother patted him on the head.

Daniel rattled off the summary of their adventure without missing a beat. "We went back in time and saw David and Goliath, and I was captured by Muslim warriors, and we saw the temple when the Romans attacked, and we shot Redcoats, and I was a little black slave for a Confederate doctor, we got to see Elijah as an old man and the bad guys were shootin' lasers at us and this little kid peed on a Kill-Bot to save Ohio!"

Elizabeth smiled at the amazing imagination of her children. "Please, breathe Daniel, breathe."

His eyes were ablaze with adventure. "It was so amazing, Mom!"

"I'm sure it was! Y'all wash your hands. Your Dad's about to come home with the Zastrows from the airport."

"Yeah! The Zastrows are coming!" Daniel shouted. He rushed onto the back porch to tell his other siblings that the Zastrows were coming over for dinner.

Charity came in the back door carrying baby Faith and the rusty musket. James entered with Elijah hanging onto his back. Daniel began to tell Grace how beautiful her granddaughter Hope Anne was in their dream, and how tasty her muffins were. That thought made him aware of how hungry he was, and he headed for the snack drawer.

Elizabeth returned to the sink full of dishes. "You'll never guess what the Zastrows have done."

Anna picked up a hand towel and began to dry the dishes that her mother had washed. "What?"

"They adopted a little girl from China, a girl that Cal saved from an abortion when he was there smuggling Bibles."

Charity put her hands on both of Anna's shoulders to look at her directly in the eye. They couldn't believe it.

Anna turned to her Mom, raised one of her reddish eyebrows higher than the other, and a curious grin shone on her face. "Please, tell me her name isn't Yoshibell."

"How'd you know?"

The end.

Or maybe not.

Other novels by this author:

The Revolt of 2020

The American Tyranny of 2020

The Uncivil War of 2020

Beating Grim

The Lesser Hills of Kinder County

Booklets available:

Ten Ways to Rock Your Wife's World

Curing the Miseries of the Mind: Depression & Anxiety

Natural Childcare in an Unnatural Age

Proofs for the Existence of God

Are There Rare Cases When Abortion Is Justified?

The Myth of Relative Morality

Sign up on Dr. Johnston's facebook page for updates on his writings and books, or visit one of his ministry websites:
www.RightRemedy.org – The Johnston Family Ministry
www.ProLifePhysicians.org – The Assn. of Pro-Life Physicians
www.PersonhoodOhio.com – Personhood Ohio
www.StopSchoolLevies.org – The Alliance to Reform Education Funding

CPSIA information can be obtained at www.ICGtesting.com
Printed in the USA
BVOW070200110412

287324BV00002B/3/P